Untouchable is a fictitious story. While the story uses some names of teams, stadiums, and media outlets that are real, even the league itself, lending the aura of authenticity to the story, the league and these teams and media entities, beyond the borrowed names, are fictitious. All characters in the story are fictitious and in no way imply a connection to any real persons associated with these teams or media organizations.

Printed in the United States by
High Command Publishing House, Inc.

ISBN: 978-1-66782-990-6

To Henri and Steven,
The greatest independent thinkers I know

UNTOUCHABLE

By

A.T. ARMADA

Chapter 1

Sometimes I wake up in the morning and feel I'm living in the land of defeat. It goes deeper than losing one's president. A while back I lost my house, my wife, and my dog in two-week's time. The house was foreclosed on due to a miscommunication with the mortgage holder. I've stuck to that story because there's a shred of truth to it. My wife of twenty-seven years walked out one morning, vowing never to return. She never has. While I was licking these wounds, Rocky was hit by a car. Not allowed to mate with his kind, he had a tendency to run wild.

But it wasn't just my life being devastated.

The country seemed to have been flipped on its head. People were calling for statues of the nation's forefathers to be pulled down. The movement to transform the face of the nation went so far as to demand its Capitol dump the name Washington for Tecumseh, a great Native American warrior.

The foundation of life was also under siege. States were now coupling men in matrimony and women were betroth-

ing women. This made no sense to me. I didn't think the government should even be involved with marriage. Beyond this, men were changing into women, by blade or creative thought, and women were growing whiskers.

Loud, dogmatic voices were shouting down all others on the Internet trying to force change on society. Being male and heterosexual had been deemed toxic by many, and being white an original sin.

Somehow, the newest pitcher in baseball had become the epicenter of all this craziness.

Then, tragedy ambushed the young hurler. This was heart-wrenching; but what the newscasters read on the air and what the papers printed churned my stomach. The Baltimore Reporter *carried the same narrative as the rest of the mainstream media with little curiosity to the possibility of malfeasance. This was despite the fact that this pitcher had become the most-hated public figure in America and many were calling out the old guillotine.*

The hate came from all sides. Women libbers hated this pitcher with a passion, though the player had been their darling at the start of all the hoopla. LGBTQ and whatever other letters piled on their hate. Trans people were beside themselves with loathing, contending several of their kind should get a chance. They wouldn't shut up.

The initial praise from people with social agendas turned to vicious condemnation. This cacophony reverber-

ating through the media and Internet was confusing even to me, given that all these loudmouths had waxed positive in the beginning when the pitcher had been called up from the minors to be given the historical shot.

The ballplayers throughout the league, though quiet at the beginning, began sniping as the season played out in the warm summer days. Even the commissioner who hailed this pitcher as baseball's savior and a hero to all, began to send mixed signals with his silence.

I took the Hoboken ferry to midtown. The Manhattan skyline and its skyscrapers were blurred, the needle of the new World Trade Center lost in the morning haze. The June sun was beginning to overpower the day at this early hour and it felt like it was going to be a hot, humid one.

The ferry lent to Hoboken's charm, making it easy to get into New York for Broadway shows and great cuisine. The ferry helped convince me to move here, though I seldom used it. I had first checked out this town while doing research on my first baseball book three years ago. Hoboken's Elysian Fields was the site of America's first organized baseball games, hosting two New York City baseball clubs in 1846. I scouted Hoboken to see what was left of the Fields. I found only a grassy meridian splitting a neighborhood street. On this strip of earth were trees, plants, and a plaque commemorating baseball's hallowed ground. Apartment buildings lined the streets on both sides of the meridian. The barroom singer Sinatra, a native son, got more respect than Elysian Fields.

It was nine a.m. and New York traffic was light, not yet rebounding fully from the pandemic. After docking at West 39th Street, I got in a cab that drove past boarded windows and empty storefronts. Park Avenue had fared no better. The cab pulled to the curb by building 245.

I was meeting with baseball's commissioner at his request. I knew him well enough to call him Jack. We first met at a sportswriter's charity dinner in Baltimore at the Camden Yards warehouse, the right field target for every slugger, located just beyond the bleachers of the ballpark. John Antonelli was the team's general manager at the time, and I was a sportswriter for the *Reporter*.

Long after leaving that paper, I wrote the book about the culture of the modern-day ballplayer, comparing it to the era when ballplayers made blue-collar wages and traveled to games on trains. When it was published, I received a letter in the mail typed under the official letterhead of the commissioner of baseball. It read, "Dear Frank, Great book," and was signed, "Jack Antonelli."

The book was on the *New York Times* best-seller list for months and was praised by critics. I wrote a second book on the impact professional sports had on the public. Once again, a critical success; but not as popular as the first because I had condemned the fans as much as I had sports management.

Ironically, the books were a ticket out of a sports world I'd come to despise: multi-millionaire crybabies who were idols to kids–and nothing but spoiled, ignorant jocks as they drove around in BMWs and Ferraris.

But the owners of the franchises were the ones I truly despised. I could not blame the players for their economic good fortune. I blamed the ones on top for ruining their sport, polluting the spectator experience and pretty much playing the fan for a sucker.

When I reached the 35ᵗʰ floor of 245 Park Avenue, I walked into a suite abuzz with baseball operations. Behind an attractive receptionist was a huge, painted mural, hitting the eye with a myriad of colors depicting a cheering crowd as a player runs toward first base. When I walked into the commissioner's office, I was immediately struck by the cold air of its air conditioning. Straight ahead he sat at a desk with sections of newspapers strewn about, and a framed photo on one side, probably of his wife, grown children, and grandchildren. There was a silver tray with a pot of coffee, two ceramic mugs, and a small plate of selected chocolates. A lone baseball rested near the tray.

He stood up tall from behind his desk. Boy, he was

in good shape. His six-foot frame was the beneficiary of running a hundred blocks each morning from his home in Cobble Hill, across the Brooklyn Bridge, and all the way to midtown.

He reached out his hand with a big smile, talking about me with the kind of respect a Godfather pulls.

"Frank Barr," he said, "since we last met you've risen to a stature in this game that surpasses even the office of the commissioner. I kiss your ring."

I knew he was laying it on thick, but still, he was the commissioner of baseball. I was smiling and speechless. After we sat down, I glanced at my left hand. I still hadn't removed the gold band.

I glanced around the room. On one wall there was a grand view of tall buildings and small cars and people below on the avenue. On the opposite wall were black and white photos of the game's past above a glass-encased display of old mitts, bats, and balls signed by Hall of Famers. An artificial pine tree stood in one corner, decorated by baseball-themed ornaments, like a year-round Christmas tree. Behind Antonelli, a big portrait of Kenesaw Mountain Landis was an imposing presence. Landis had banned eight White Sox players for fixing the 1919 World Series even though a court had acquitted them of wrongdoing. With one edict, he had made baseball honest again. So far, this commissioner has seemed as bold and decisive.

"Please," he said, pointing to the tray, "have some dark chocolate and coffee. My energy boost in the morning." He poured out some coffee.

"Your *Game of Catch* was outstanding. I've read it twice," he said. "The second book was spot on. It took us all to task, but we needed it. We're all a bunch of corrupt pretenders."

I felt a writer's power surge through me, hearing that my work had such impact. I wanted to run out onto the streets of New York right then, and with notepad and pen, find a park bench and start writing another book. Ideas were always swirling in my head. Now that I had the luxury of time that success brought, I had a notion for the next Great American Novel.

"I could have called any of a dozen sportswriters to cover this," Antonelli was saying, "but the moment calls for some depth from an extraordinary writer."

Antonelli was the first person of renown who spoke such words to my face. When praise came my way, it was usually from written reviews on the books.

As I bit into a chunk of dark chocolate, I wondered why he had called me here. On the phone, he only said he wanted to discuss an important event.

After his recent proposal for the leagues to do away with all interleague and interdivision play, I had a premonition someday the commissioner and I would talk about this. Idiocy among the owners had killed the pennant race. For me, it had been the crime of the century.

"Frank," he said, still warming up to the purpose at hand, "we are living in momentous times.

"Things are happening today we would never have imagined fifty years ago. Who would have thought, when you and I were kids, someday we'd be watching any game we wanted on a smartphone?

"Who would have thought we'd see the day," he said, frowning, "American League teams would be playing National League teams before the season got to the World Series?"

Then he gave me a nod by misquoting a line out of my book that characterized interleague games, "It's like one league pissing on another's sovereignty; a nation's army crossing the borders of another country." The hyperbole was mine, but I would never write a vulgar word.

Antonelli had promised to bring back the season-long excitement of the old pennant race. It sounded like he was serious about it. In those days, a fan was familiar with all the players in the league and enjoyed perusing the standings and box scores each morning over a cup of coffee.

"Momentous times, Frank ... can any event be bigger than China?" he asked rhetorically.

He grabbed the ball on his desk and tossed it to me. Turning it in my hand, I saw it had been signed in hanzi with blue ink. The artistic Chinese characters may have spelled the name of a personage, maybe the chairman of China's communist party, or maybe it was a proverb. I chose not to inquire right then and tossed the ball back.

I did wonder what the commissioner was driving at.

He had led baseball into unchartered territory by inking the deal with China just a year ago. The venture opened up a huge, exotic market on the mainland, and helped the party's rulers revive the game.

My instincts, however, told me the grand design ran counter to the intent of reverting the majors to its original structure.

Two of our minor-league teams had already flown to Beijing and Shanghai this spring and played the home clubs of those cities. Four major-league teams would be there in August to play out a week of the regular schedule. Chinese teams may eventually be accepted into the majors. Still, Antonelli was calling baseball back to a time when teams played only within their respective leagues; when each game mattered, and teams would rise and fall in the standings every day; creating the daily fan and making for a suspenseful season.

Maybe he recognized his strategy going forward needed some fine tuning. I would give him an earful if he called on my counsel.

Antonelli rocked back and forth in his leather chair, a square jaw and broad shoulders denoting his manly presence. His voice on the other hand was distinctively boyish, though mature in the deliberate way he delivered his words.

"China is big; but this is bigger than the Jackie Robinson story," he said. "And that was a story of an entire race."

The reason I sat before him continued to come in and out of focus.

"This story isn't about creating equality for a race, or a gender, as some people make it out to be. No!" The Commissioner slammed his fist down on the desk; the black suspenders quivered over his starched white shirt.

Histrionics aside, what was he saying?

He stood up.

"No. This is a story in defense of the so-called patriarchy under attack in this country. More than that, it's about what it is to be a man and a woman.

"Frank, I want a writer familiar with the sport, sure; but I need someone with a greater sense of what this moment is about. That's why I want you." He sat again.

I listened, perplexed. I had heard only vague rumors. My head was spinning with all his hyperbole and contradictions.

"Frank," Antonelli said, speaking in more of a low-key manner while taking a sip of coffee from his mug, "a girl named Greta Reich will take the mound this Sunday down in Baltimore against New York. I need you to cover Reich's first game."

The commissioner paused for effect. My thoughts raced to comprehend the meaning of his words. The mound–what? He didn't say home plate. Of the possible events playing in my mind, one was the first female umpire to call balls and strikes.

But sending a girl to the mound?

I felt like I was on a carnival ride, questions popping up and passing in a blur.

"When you get down there, Gazzetti will arrange things for you. You will have all the clearance you need to cover her, and the game."

So, the reason he called on me was a dish that was not cooked in his kitchen, but one prepared in his old office by Baltimore's current GM. Evidently it was a gambit the commissioner wanted to capitalize on.

"In many ways," he said, reaching again for the baseball and weighing it in his hand, "this is bigger than China."

He leaned forward. "You've got carte blanche. Exclusive pre-game, post-game interviews–whatever you want," he said. "You'll have exclusives in the *Times* and

Sports Illustrated. Then I want you to write a book about the season. I want everything you write to be read not only by baseball fans, but by the world. I want a book out this winter. Your book, any way you want to write it.

"Are you interested?"

Chapter 2

I took the Amtrak down to Baltimore the next morning. The train rumbled over the tracks past blue-collar backyards with shirts and pants hanging from clotheslines. I thought of the pennants that hang in baseball parks denoting championship seasons. It had been a long time since Baltimore had won it all. I contemplated the team's pitching staff and the current struggle to win games.

The train crossed Main Streets of old towns and ran along highways and over rivers, passing through the grandeur of the Delaware and Susquehanna. I thought of the big town the train was heading toward and the neighborhoods I knew intimately. I was ambivalent about returning to the place that would evoke poignant memories, yet thrilled with the opportunity the commissioner gave me. A stab at the next Great American Novel would wait. I began considering how to approach the assignment.

I had not fully formed my own opinion on what was

about to transpire. A woman behind the plate shouting strike three to a man would be progress enough to my way of thinking. I could not fathom how it could be a woman was being handed a ball to pitch a game. I had my prejudiced viewpoints, but I was totally in the dark with no information to enlighten me.

I jotted notes on who I should interview. John Ralston was Baltimore's manager. It was rumored he wasn't thrilled with his boss foisting baseball's first female player on him.

His boss, General Manager Phil Gazzetti, would be interesting. From what I'd read in the morning's papers, he was fashioning himself in the media as the moment's Branch Rickey. Rickey had brought black players into the majors by signing Jackie Robinson to play for the Brooklyn Dodgers. He shrewdly assessed the talent pool in the Negro Leagues, and saw no reason why the Dodgers shouldn't pull from it.

The circumstances around the signing of Greta Reich had no similarities to that time. There were no female baseball leagues. No one saw potential in females playing baseball and certainly not in a male league. Greta Reich was a stunt. That's how I took the news when I heard it.

Gazzetti was taking a page from Bill Veeck, famous for his promotional prowess. Veeck, who owned the St. Louis Browns, sent a three-foot, seven-inch midget to the plate to pinch hit during an August doubleheader. I was prepared to cover a carnival act in Baltimore.

Besides Gazzetti, I would want to interview the team's catcher who would be guiding Reich on every pitch. I would want to see also how the other infielders responded to her.

Not least of all I would interview the scout who had touted Reich to Gazzetti. What was this clown about?

I walked into the lounge car and found a copy of the *Baltimore Sun*. There were a few articles referring to Sunday's game, but not one revealing anything about Reich. There was a great satirical piece about a woman on the mound and how she might show empathy for the disadvantaged batter at the plate. I chuckled, and wondered about my coverage of the coming game. If Reich was an empath, and was yanked in the first inning after giving up twenty runs, I might have to resort to humor myself.

When my train eased into Baltimore's Penn's Station on North Charles Street, I sensed the ghost of my past life. I had taken the train many times to D.C., Philly, and New York to cover games or escape town with my wife. I strode through the station and threw my suit bag into the back of a green cab. I told the driver, "Waterfront Hotel." I knew the visiting team was also staying at the Waterfront. I would be looking for chances to bump into players, hoping to get their take on the "historic" game this Sunday.

My cab driver was a big, broad-shouldered man with a thick accent. I learned he was from Georgia, near Russia. I fished for some lowdown on what fans thought. "Any hubbub about the big game on Sunday?"

"Hubbub. What you mean, hubbub?"

"What's the buzz? You know, what's the feeling around town about the new pitcher?"

"Ahhh," he said, intoning his awareness of the subject. "You Americans."

He glanced at me in the rearview mirror with sympathy in his eyes, a touch of contempt in his voice. "You Americans," he repeated, saying nothing more until we turned off the street and onto the hotel driveway.

I checked into the Waterfront. In my room there was a tray of chocolate strawberries, a small bottle of cognac, and a welcoming note signed by the hotel's manager. It was the corporate, personal touch of a class hotel, though I would never meet the guy or hear from him again. The sweeping view of the Inner Harbor from my window I took as a salute from the commissioner. At Antonelli's behest the team was putting me up, seeing to it I got first-cabin treatment.

I called the team's front office and was put through to the GM's assistant. Phil Gazzetti was expecting my call.

"I'm having lunch for us sent to my office suite at the

Yards. I look forward to catching up with you," he said in a raspy voice I remembered well.

Gazzetti was a hot shot, cocky as a rooster. Five-foot, nine-inches tall, he displayed an energy and ambition as subtle as an old steam locomotive. We were both covering sports for the *Reporter* before he left to join the team's front office. He made it clear to everyone around him he aspired to be a general manger with a major league team. After a year managing ticket sales he got his break with a promotion as a liaison to the minor league affiliates and eventually was involved with player contracts, reporting to the GM, Antonelli at the time. When Antonelli was made commissioner by baseball's team-owners Gazzetti was given the chance at his dream. From my many conversations with him at the *Reporter*, I was sure the club's owner, Ed Farley, loved his pep and constant talk of getting to the World Series.

Gazzetti's enthusiasm was only marred by a penchant for giving spotty talent a shot in the bigs, seeing some quirk of character he thought could help win games. I recall how he had touted Whittle Jones. A utility infielder, Jones was known to sit before his locker whittling a small block of balsa to calm his nerves before a game. Whittle was actually his christened name. With Gazzetti behind him he had the makings of a folk hero. He could run and steal a base if he could get on. Gazzetti saw him as a sleeper, a winner ready to break out and spark the team to the Series. But he was no better than a .200 hitter. After one of his strikeouts he disappeared into the clubhouse where the bench coach found him whittling on his balsa wood. Gazzetti included him in a multi-player trade a month later.

It took me five minutes by cab to reach the ballpark. Once inside the old Camden Yards warehouse, I took an elevator to the second floor and found his suite. I met his secretary stationed outside his door, a young, slim red-head who showed me in.

The GM's office had a sweeping view of the ballpark. It looked over the brick concourse that fans and food vendors made festive as a game was being played. The green outfield grass, the tan diamond, the forest green seats, and the bleachers were all empty right now. The *Baltimore Sun* logo towered alone behind the bleachers.

I felt a tinge of pride gazing at the *Sun* logo. It had a black and white, line-art design featuring old modes of transportation from trains to sailing ships, and a woman and an eagle prominent. For twenty years I had covered sports for the *Reporter,* the town's underdog newspaper that competed with the *Sun* with a staff a quarter of its size. The talk around town often gave the *Reporter* higher grades on its sports coverage. Looking at the *Sun* logo brought back those feelings when we outdid the big guy.

I ended up leaving the paper for a marketing position that doubled my salary. Then I ventured on my own, starting up a T-shirt company, using my contacts with the city's sports franchises to get premium contracts with the town's stadiums and arenas. That company earned me a modest living on tight margins, but I never liked dealing with all the details it took to run the operation in the black. I sold the business for a small sum when I left town.

Gazzetti was dressed like he was fully enjoying his stature as GM of a major league team. He wore cufflinks. You might wear cufflinks in New York, but Baltimore was a small city without New York's killer career-culture. In Baltimore you could make a true friend; in New York friends kept tabs on favors rendered for one's standing in the city's dog-eat-dog world. In short, the cufflinks probably impressed no one in Baltimore but Gazzetti himself, feeding his self-image as the next Branch Rickey.

Phil came out from behind his wide, cherry wood desk and strutted up to me with abbreviated steps, pressing his shoes into the carpet much like a batter digs in, testing the dirt beneath his cleats. He hadn't changed too much since I'd last seen him, maybe a bit paunchier, and still flashing his know-it-all smile. No one could ever win an argument with the guy when we were both at the *Reporter*.

After we shook hands we small-talked a few minutes. "It seems you're always in the thick of things," I told him, alluding to the big event I was there to cover. He flashed a self-congratulatory grin, then spoke on my success as a book author.

"You were always a little too deep for me, Barr. Your books are right there on my shelf. I'm not sure Farley appreciated them," Gazzetti said with a knowing grin. "In some quarters, you're as popular as Jim Bouton was with *Ball Four*," referring to the old-timer who wrote a tell-all book about his Yankee teammates, not much appreciated by them.

Gazzetti led me over to the big, wide window that looked out over the ballfield.

"Come Sunday," he said, "we'll be making baseball history. Hell, we'll be making American history."

"World history," I added, just to fan the flames of his ego.

"We'll watch together from our skybox," he said, nodding and grinning.

"I suppose I have just one question beforehand," I told him.

He eyed me with hospitable patience. "Shoot."

"Can she pitch?"

"What?" he bristled. "You think I'd bring her up here if she couldn't compete with the boys? Well, you just watch. Judge for yourself."

Chapter 3

I was able to ambush one of New York's hurlers inside the Waterfront on Friday afternoon, knuckleballer Siegfried Franz. On the stool next to him was Rudy Smith, the first baseman and slugger who struck out three times the number of homers he hit. They were both eating a late lunch at the bar. I had frequented it during my *Reporter* days when it allowed cigar smoking. I told these young men I was on special assignment for the commissioner to cover Sunday's game and Greta Reich's debut.

"I'd appreciate it if you could give me some comments, on or off the record."

"I'm ready for her," Rudy Smith said as he chomped on his Reuben sandwich somewhere in the midst of his bushy red beard. "Don't care how pretty she be, won't let it distract me. Give me your best pitch."

There was a rumor circulating that Greta Reich was "hot;" but at the clubhouse later that day one player said she was a "scag." There were no pictures or videos of her yet. She didn't even have a social media page. She had pitched minor league ball somewhere in the southeast under the name, G. Reich, the publicist never letting out the new pitcher was a female. Maybe she wore a short haircut and was flat-chested. It would have been possible to hide her sex. Whatever local press came around was not allowed to interview or photograph her. Rumors had begun, spun no doubt by her teammates; but then she was called up, coinciding with Gazzetti's press announcement that baseball was about to break the gender barrier.

No one in town had seen her yet.

"Look, it's a long way from the mound to the plate," Franz said, eyeing me, as if unsure I had ever seen a live ballgame. "If you don't have the physical stature, no gal is going to overpower a male batter. So, I don't know what game Gazzetti has up his sleeve. Hey, maybe she has a hell of a knuckleball." He started to bite into his sandwich but paused, saying, "Hey, maybe she's got balls."

It was uncharacteristic for a Yankee to make off-color comments to a writer. Members of that team faithfully played the role of goodwill ambassadors for the game; they were always polite and proper. Franz's remark would make good ink, but he had said it without rancor. It would not appear in anything I would write.

I headed for the visitor's clubhouse a bit later, looking to get into off-the-cuff conversations with more players about their expectations for Sunday's game. The players milled in and out, taking off street clothes and dressing up in gray uniforms, some wandering into the trainer's room, or the hospitality room for a bite of food. When I mentioned Greta Reich most of them gave me a chilly "no comment," and one of the New York relievers said, "What the f— was Gazzetti thinking? But it will be interesting as she gets clobbered. Look, that's off the record."

In the home clubhouse, I walked over to the locker with the ceramic Buddha wired to its door. Baltimore's catcher hadn't shown yet, or was being worked on in the training room. He was probably the most curious of the team's characters.

None of the players wanted their comments or attitudes reaching the front office or the public. They knew how the PC-police culture could derail their careers, even get one suspended.

Gazzetti told me he thought she was arriving on a late-night train, only hours before she was to pitch. "She likes to be mysterious," he said. "Best interview her after the game." He said he was keeping her under wraps. "She should feel no media pressure before she has the chance to show her stuff."

"When you meet her," Gazzetti said, "you'll understand why I took this approach. For one thing, she's very shy."

While Greta Reich was kept distant from the press, the media whipped up its own hoopla over the event like it had never done before. Without being fed much, it played up the mystery angle. Where she had pitched and where she was from, how she was, and her vital statistics remained a secret. The subject of Eddie Gaedel, the midget who had pinch hit that one August game for the St. Louis Browns, was often referred to. "Would this too be a Veeckian stunt?" they asked.

Meanwhile feminists were having at it, hailing Greta as America's next Amelia Earhart, painting a legend of a heroine who dared ascend to a man's realm. "Diamonds Are a Girl's Best Friend," a music video going viral on the Internet, was shot on a baseball diamond. The action showed a male player being tagged out by a girl with long blond hair flowing from the cap, struck out by a curvy pitcher wearing a skirt, and a fielder being spiked by a ponytailed player sliding into second base.

Because the media was cued to the story but days before the big game, there was a rush to play it up. Countless articles and interviews blitzed across newspapers and television screens expounding on sport and physical anatomy and the prospects of a female pitcher blowing the ball by a major league batter. Historical footage of the girl league that played in place of the majors during World War II was seen everywhere. The Hollywood version, *A League of Their Own*, had a quick revival. There were all kinds of videos on the Internet trying to be funny, one showing a pitcher with high heels getting stuck in the dirt mound.

After a bit of lobbying by the commissioner, CBS was going to broadcast the game to the nation and CNN would carry the game to the world. Everyone who wanted to would be able to see the game.

That night, as I slipped into the hotel bed and snuggled into a pillow, I thought about which seat and from what angle I would want to watch her pitch.

Imagining this mystery pitcher on a mound, my thoughts meandered to the one time I played catch with my wife in our small backyard. She threw and caught, lobster-like, claws flailing clumsily until the ball glanced off the top of her glove and struck her nose.

I still could not divorce us in my mind's eye, three years now since we split: still saw us strolling neighborhood streets or sitting shoulder to shoulder at ballgames. I saw us hammering away at crab shells inside Obrycki's off Fells Point, her lusty laughter filling the room. We had no children. With no one to distract us we spent most of our free time hand in hand.

In time, the romance disappeared. It never registered with me that we were tilting away from each other. The newspaper job was demanding but she never got jealous or suspicious when late game-nights or road trips kept me from her; I chalked this up to her devotion. When she wanted more space and insisted on a king-size bed, putting me an arms-length away, I chalked it up to an aging libido. Then, without any forewarning, she just got up and left me for an old flame who owns dozens of houses on the Maryland shore. I chalked that up to plain arithmetic. She was kind enough to leave me our house that was in foreclosure.

I turned over in the bed several times. Finally, I reached up, turned on the lamp and looked down on my left hand. I tugged a bit on the ring until it slid off my finger. I relegated it to the wallet where it would still be close.

Funny, I've often wondered if the hardball she took on the nose had been the beginning of the end. Maybe I threw it too hard. It was just one of the things I look back on that could have been different.

One can bury the pain but not the regret, it seemed, like a batter who swings at a pitch straight down the middle and misses, ending the game.

It was near midnight. I got up out of bed, threw on a pair of jeans and a pale green T-shirt and took the elevator down to the lobby. I walked through the adjacent lobby passing sofas and chairs and into the bar. It was full of people: the night's game would have finished and there were probably some fans and players in the room. I sniffed the smell of alcohol, listened to the noise of all the chatter and walked out, not up for it.

I walked back into the main lobby and looked around. There were two young women at the check-in counter, each talking separately to hotel clerks. One of the women wore a short black dress and black high heels. She was blond with a cut that revealed her ears and the nape of her neck. She was short. The other girl had light brown hair with a more boyish haircut. It was tapered and bristly. She wore tight jeans and tan converse sneakers. She was lanky, maybe five foot, nine inches tall, long arms hanging at her sides. She turned from the counter, hung a suit bag over the shoulder and down her back and headed to the elevator alcove. The shorter one soon followed pulling a small suitcase on wheels and displaying a lot of thigh in her walk. I guessed she was an airline flight attendant.

I walked over to the check-in counter. I spoke to one of the ladies behind it, a young Filipina. "Hi," I said, smiling. "Could you tell me if Greta Reich has checked in yet?"

"I'm sorry, it's not our policy to give out such information at the front desk. You could go to a house phone and ask for her if you'd like."

I thought it was too late to be talking to this mystery pitcher if she was in her room. I would wait until after the game for the interview that Gazzetti set up.

I took the elevator up to my floor and went back to bed.

Chapter 4

Sunday morning, I was up early and walking through the Inner Harbor over to Federal Hill, one of my old haunts. It was a crisp, clear, sunny June morning. The morning walk was my answer to the commissioner's run from Brooklyn to midtown, but without the sweat or push. I hadn't run in years.

The temperature was supposed to get up to eighty-five. I walked over to the Cross Street Market and inside to the fish bar. I ordered the grilled shrimp and wanted a draft to go with the salty Cajun seasoning, but thought better of it. I wanted my head to be clear for the game. I had learned in covering the team in the old days that just one beer could dull the senses to the point of not caring if you missed a pitch, a play, or a home run. Even when I would watch a game on a day off, I enjoyed the game better sober.

At the rounded end of the horseshoe bar, a blond-haired, grisly faced young man was eating his breakfast with his girlfriend, drinking a beer. I called over to him,

"Hey, great morning."

"I'll drink to it," he said, raising his mug.

"What's going on at the ballpark today? I understand they're trotting out a female pitcher," I said, throwing out some bait to see what kind of comments I would catch.

"Yeah! What's that about? I don't know, man. She better have some kind of English on the ball."

"You don't have to be fast to be a good pitcher," the girlfriend threw in.

"Are you guys going to the game?" I asked.

"Nah. We're Ravens fans. We thought about going just for the novelty of it. But I figured she's gonna get sent to the showers in the first inning. Tickets aren't cheap."

I went back along the Harbor to the Waterfront, showered, and got myself prepared to cover the game. All I needed was a note pad and pen, a scorecard, and my smartphone. Its pictures were sharp enough for use in print articles. Its recorder good enough for interviews, audio or video. My style was not to be too engrossed in the process of recording everything. I wanted my own eyes, ears, and mind to take everything in and think about what I was experiencing. I would jot down just brief notes. I threw on a fresh pair of jeans, a plain forest green t-shirt cut with a breast pocket. I also carried my laptop in my knapsack in case at some point I availed myself of the press box. I was sure I would find some old friends there.

I had called Gazzetti to see if he could get me a pass that would allow me to roam the stadium for any empty seat I could find. I picked it up from the ticket window along with a pass that would get me into the press box. The first pitch would be thrown at one o'clock, but I got there early.

The Eutaw Street concourse was filling up already with the early-birders stuffing their mouths by the grills. I strode past them, looking past the bleachers onto the field where players were shagging fly balls in the out-field. A glimpse of this action still gave me a thrill.

Inside, I found a seat by the rail on the first base side. One of the coaches, a former second baseman who had played for Baltimore ten years ago, was engaged in a game of pepper, stroking the ball into the ground with a bat to a few players twenty feet or so before him. Another coach was hitting high flies to the outfield with a fungo bat. Soon, a pitcher walked to the mound behind a net to throw batting practice. Players began taking their turns at cuts on the balls thrown in a loose, easy manner to the plate.

There was a time I loved this early pre-game activity. I remember when my father took me to Yankee Stadium back in the time of Mantle and Maris. When I got inside the Stadium, I was awed. Seeing Mickey and Roger bat was a special moment. They were men to me with God-like powers. We went to several games in those years and would arrive early enough to catch batting practice and see a lot of balls rocketed into the stands, even the stadium's upper deck. Recognizing the players by their stances at the plate, how they threw the ball, how they ran, provided a magical experience for a young fan. There was the energy of motion of these men in uniform, and yet a relaxed atmosphere as they warmed up on the field.

Then baseball's karma was attacked by commercialism, greed, and stupidity. Big screens went up in most of the parks high beyond the outfield seats. Video commercials played on them with noise and moving images distracting one from the treasure of the game, everything that it was as a balm against the hectic, modern world. The character of the players and the game itself began to disintegrate before all the commercialism and electronic wizardry. People paid for tickets to see baseball and were force-fed television and rock music between innings, even between pitches and, worst of all, during pre-game warmups and batting practice. My memories of how it used to be were like far-out dreams of paradise, never to be appreciated again or even understood by succeeding generations.

I sat in my seat looking out to the *Sun* logo above the centerfield bleachers and the brick warehouse beyond right field. Players jogged, sprinted, and chased balls on the field, now and then glancing up to video commotion on the big screen, usually a car commercial. I sat trying to enjoy the pregame activity in spite of all the distraction. I tried to keep a positive frame of mind to override my grudge against the powers that be in baseball.

I looked out beyond the outfield where pitchers were warming up. I tried to see the player I had come to watch but I was too far from the outfield bullpen. Two right-handed pitchers were warming up, then one of them walked away. At the time, it looked like the ball boy had taken his place, throwing left-handed pitches to the catcher.

Then on the big screen a scene from *A League of Their Own* was playing, an intense, competitive scene on the ballfield. What the hell was Gazzetti doing? I figured all the players were cussing him out under their breath. This was the major leagues. This was hardball the way the game was designed to be played. You got a female player who can compete, let's see her. Don't show the girls who could never have been on the same field with the men. As Tom Hanks said in the movie: "there's no crying in baseball." Well, there are no skirts either ... but girls in skirts were playing ball on the big screen.

I was self-aware enough to know I had a prejudice against women in baseball. It was a man's game as far as

I was concerned. To play the game you had to be tough. The field was a challenging run for anyone. The diamond was large: running on it with any speed took a lot of conditioning–and the ground could be unforgiving. The dirt of the diamond was packed down. At best, you scraped your thighs sliding into a base; at worst, you broke an ankle. Fielders got their shins and thighs ripped up by incoming, high cleats. Batters faced the possibility of being killed with each pitch.

When a boy was a little leaguer, he could dream and pretend to be a major leaguer, and still be a boy. When he got older and ran onto a big-league field the game forced him then to become a man. I remembered those years well. Those who could not live up to the demands of the game on the big field, or stand at the plate to face intimidating pitchers, left the game. Those who gave it up became fans who appreciated what the game exacted both physically and mentally from playing it.

I looked back out to the bullpen. No action. Now New York was taking the field for batting practice.

Chapter 5

I wasn't against Greta Reich pitching in a major league game this Sunday afternoon. I didn't expect it would go well for her, and I suspected Phil Gazzetti's motives were not in the game's best interest. If she turned out to have pitching prowess, I was all for giving her a shot. In spite of my belief that it was a man's game, I relished the idea of a woman pricking the balloon of the male egos in baseball. They were spoiled brats who talked about being entertainers as if they aspired to become movie actors or rock stars. If Greta Reich turned out to be a stunt, then the players were getting what they deserved: a chance to be on stage with this blockbuster act, egos be damned. If Reich could hold her own on the mound she would earn my respect.

When I had left my temporary box seat for the press box to see some of my old cohorts in the sportswriting world, I found Rolly Singer at his laptop with an unlit pipe in his mouth. He was still with the *Baltimore Sun*. He had not aged well, obesity accelerating the process. After searching his face for remnants of his youth, I gave up and adjusted to Rolly's new look. We shook hands, shared some stories and came around to the topic of the day.

"You think she can pitch?" I asked Singer, knowing at this point he could only guess.

"Doesn't matter. Everybody's making money over this. The park will be filled. The ratings will go through the roof. You and I will each get a book out of it; who cares if she can pitch."

Well, I thought, maybe Gazzetti. Or maybe not.

As I looked out over the field I noticed a cluster of pink hats in the bleachers. Women libbers no doubt.

When one p.m. approached I headed back down to the field level. I sought the same area I had sat in earlier. It seemed full, but I thought maybe some season ticket holders wouldn't show up. Baseball today had an elite, casual fan base: interested and wealthy enough to buy season tickets, but not interested enough to go to every game. Somebody would have made other plans.

There were two empty seats several rows down from the one I had and closer toward home plate.

As the managers gathered with the chief umpire at the plate, I took one of those seats. An usher approached me soon after and I showed her my pass. She took it, read it, nodded, and said, "Enjoy the game."

The public address announcer, a female voice, was

welcoming the fans as the players were running out onto the field to cheers from the crowd. The first baseman, Zorro Negrewski, began slinging grounders to the infield. Catcher Monk Morton was standing behind home plate. Finally, a very short person, slight of shoulder, was walking in demure fashion toward the mound. The number on the player's back was zero. A mitt hung, drooped and swinging from the right hand. The left hand was slinking beside the left leg, turning slightly inward along with the hip on each step. Beneath the purple cap were wisps of short blonde hair by the ears and the nape of the neck. The head was held up, seeming to appraise the players in the field. Monk Morton squatted behind the plate when number zero reached the mound. The umpire threw the pitcher a new ball and I noticed the stadium noise had converted to a dead silence.

The silence turned to murmurs and the buzz of chatter as the pitcher started warming up, rearing back from the rubber, winding and throwing. That's when I noticed the bareness of the leg and rump revealed by the wide slit up the uniform trousers of her right leg. She would wind and then pivot way around toward first base, then kick her right leg high like a ballet dancer before coming back to the ground with the right foot as her left arm and hand delivered the ball across home plate. Most of the warm up pitches looked off-speed with little velocity. Her grandiose wind-up gave her a commanding stature that belied her actual height, which, according to the game's program, was normal for a woman.

At that moment, I heard several people to my left, right, and behind me, saying, "She's only five foot, three inches tall!"

She would have looked even shorter, take away the mound.

The novelty of the historic moment sunk in as I watched her standing on the rubber under the cap with the initials, BC, embroidered on its crest. I watched her take about ten warm-up tosses. None of them had much velocity. Meanwhile I was mesmerized by her exhibitionism, in both her style of movement on the mound and her decidedly female presence. I wondered who put her up to playing in trousers that could be mistaken for a stripper's get-up. The slit along the side of her right trouser leg began above the knee and widened as it made its way up to the flank of her rump so that her flesh there was like a magnet to the eyes. The parting of her pants up along the leg was hemmed in the team's purple color with black trim, just like the lettering on the shirt. There were purple stripes running down the legs of the players' uniforms. Greta had the stripe on her left leg; on her right, the slit seemed to have split the stripe. One could say it was tastefully done. It triggered the imagination more than anything. Still, I wondered who had decided to make her uniform sexy.

I was debating with myself if this bit of tease had any place on an athletic field. Usually, any risqué element to a female athlete's garb seemed to be for the sake of liberating her motion. But I thought of a figure skater's dress. The men wore slacks, the women itsy bitsy skirts. Besides I was being won over by Greta Reich's shape and flash of flesh as she wound around and kicked up that leg, pointing it to first base before raising it high as she spun toward the plate and came down with the throw. I liked ample thighs in a woman.

This was the first time I was observing a pitcher's motion with lustful eyes.

To add more unmistakable feminine presence on the mound, the top two buttons of her shirt were free of the button holes, revealing some more white flesh. The male in me hadn't died. I began to hope she would defy all odds and overcome the batters that were eager, no doubt, to clobber her.

Chapter 6

The first baseman rolled his practice ball toward the dugout. Reich threw a final warm-up toss and Monk Morton threw the ball to the shortstop at second base, who shuffled it to the second baseman, who side-armed it to the third baseman. The third baseman, Jake Fielder, stood super erect and threw the ball to his pitcher. None of the fielders were talking, and I noticed that none were talking to her. Morton stayed squatting behind the plate. There was no customary jaunt to the mound to confer with his pitcher before the action began. Maybe he had sunk into meditation in his squat. I wondered how this peace-loving Buddhist reconciled the violence that occasionally came his way at the plate. He sat back placidly.

Reich was clearly on her own.

The usual din from the stands was subdued in anticipation of the first pitch. I wondered if the crowd would get behind her or if they were turned off by the whole proposition, with the slit up her side being the exclamation point.

The batter was Todd Allston, the New York short-stop, a lean, athletic young man who had hit for a low average his first three years up from the minors, but got on base a lot by waiting on the pitcher and playing for the walk. Reich brought her arms, mitt and ball to her chest, stepped back to spin into her grand wind-up and flung the ball in a very fluid manner to the plate. Compared to the usual pitch in the majors it seemed like slow motion. It was a low off-speed pitch and Allston lunged his swing, got a piece of it, but the ball dribbled slowly to the third baseman. Fielder played it cleanly into his glove and fired hard to Negrewski for the first out of the game. The crowd released some cheers and applause but it wasn't clear if it was for Reich or just for the home team starting the game on the right foot.

The next batter was Ted Cook, the second baseman. Cook was a solid hitter. He had a formidable stance, waving the bat about his head in a menacing way. Reich wound and threw. The ball had a little bit more velocity than before but seemed low and just off the outside corner but Cook went after it and hit a weak grounder to second base. Riobonito swept it up and tossed it to Negrewski. Two down.

The crowd was more pumped in its response. I'm sure most in the crowd were thinking it would be great if she retired the side in order.

The throng of humanity in the park was enthralled by the presence of a short creature on the mound, a rare sight. The fact that this creature was in command and was a woman was a first in baseball history.

Walking to the plate was the bearded first baseman I chatted with at the Waterfront bar, Rudy Smith. He was the first left-handed batter Reich faced. With the first pitches to Smith, I began to understand that her fluid motion and release of the ball was deceptive if not overpowering. Her left-hand tosses came slowly spinning its way to the plate, slowly compared to usual major league pitching speeds; but she was handcuffing Smith, who was clearly trying to pull the ball over the right field wall. He swung so hard you knew he was trying to send the ball crashing through a Camden Yards warehouse window.

The count was two and two. Her next pitch was a slow roundhouse curve that dipped low beyond the outside corner of the plate. Smith tried holding back his swing and pulling the bat back, but the ump called strike three. Greta Reich had retired the side and the stadium erupted in approval. I looked all around at the full house, the fans standing and cheering. For the moment, baseball was a great game again. I was a helpless romantic and this historic inning was full of sweeping emotions, even to one who saw the unvarnished truth about the game's decay.

For a second I wondered what my ex-wife was doing. We had gone to many games together, and she loved to root for the home team. But my eyes were on Reich's walk toward me and the dugout. I got a good glimpse of her face. It seemed intent on staying in the game to face more New York batters. It also looked boyishly cute: but the baseball cap helped lend that impression.

I heard loud cheers from the bleachers. The women in the pink caps were still standing, and now raising a banner that read: "Castrate Those Batters, Greta!"

Ok, typical of today's women libbers. I sat down and found the ballgame broadcast on my smart phone. I wanted to hear how they were rehashing baseball's historic inning.

"No doubt about it, New York's batters were pulled off-stride. We'll see how she does as the game progresses. Did she out-finesse them so far, Paul? Or are we watching a game where a subpar player is bringing the level of play down to her level–dare I say it–to a girl's game?"

"Yeah, but she doesn't throw like a girl, Smokey. She's throwing like a real pitcher."

"As the Yankees take the field I want to welcome to the booth, Beth Frye, president of the W.U.F., Women United Forever. Welcome to the booth, Beth."

"Good to be here, Smokey."

"You must have been thrilled by Greta Reich's facing down the first three men at the plate."

"She outsmarted them. She strung out their egos and clipped off their wahoos! Hah!" She delivered this presumably humorous line with a humorless voice.

"I guess that's one way of putting it. Did you think she'd do so well?"

"Well, no one knew or knows anything about her right now. To be honest, who knew what to expect. But it shouldn't surprise anyone that given a chance, a woman can compete with any man in a sport where intelligence is used–and not just strength or speed. In time, women can take on men in those arenas as well; but they've been physically conditioned for hundreds of years to perform tasks that don't stretch their abilities. But brains? Women can outsmart men any day of the week!"

I was growing disgusted. The first inning wasn't over and the broadcasters had already let politics into the game. W.U.F. no less. Beth Frye was a man-hater going back three decades.

Come on Smokey, send her back to the bleachers.

Baltimore loaded the bases in the bottom half of the inning but couldn't bring a run across the plate. The long inning served to create a building anticipation of how Reich would fare when she took to the mound again. Or would the skipper over-manage and pull Reich from the game after one inning. It wouldn't surprise me if Gazzetti had instructed this before the game. Doing so would create a great deal of expectation for her second appearance, but at the risk of robbing the fans in the seats on this Sunday afternoon. Or Reich could disappear forever into baseball folklore, and Gazzetti would be famous forever after for this one inning.

Negrewski was rolling grounders to the infield but the pitcher hadn't walked to the mound yet. The umpire, a burly man in blue short sleeves and gray pants walked toward the dugout when Reich came out onto the playing field, walking in no hurry to what had become the center of the universe.

Morton trotted to the mound to have a few words with his pitcher for the first time in the game. Reich's diminutive presence on the field was stark with Morton standing over her.

Had Reich been pitching sixty years ago she would have stood nine inches taller on the rubber; but the mound had been shaved down since to six inches above home plate level so pitchers could not have too much advantage. I don't know if a taller mound would have helped her. She seemed to have her own advantage of throwing the ball on a low plane that batters were not accustomed to. So far, her pitches came in from a three-quarter arm motion or side-armed off her high kick at a plane a foot or more below that of the average major league pitcher. Her throws also dipped slightly as they reached the plate.

On top of that, the hitters so far had not adjusted to her speed. They were trained to react to balls coming in at ninety to a hundred miles per hour. Reich's came in slower than the average slow pitcher.

After several warm-up tosses, the clean-up hitter stepped to the plate, Wilson Clan, a young black man who refused to respond to liberal commentators who pestered him about considering a name change. Clan hit for high average and power. He took a big sweeping swing at Reich's first pitch, which dropped at the plate like a yo-yo. His swing was way out ahead of the pitch.

Reich stood on the rubber, her left hand holding the ball inside the mitt resting by her chest. She was looking at Monk Morton's signs, his fingers flashing between his legs, crouched behind home plate. She was slightly shaking her head every two seconds. Finally, she nodded and began her wind up. Her second pitch showed something new. It went straight to the catcher's mitt and Clan waited for it, and swung for the fences. But the ball hopped up as he swung, lifting a high fly to center field that was an easy out.

The fifth and sixth batters in the Yankee order grounded out on the first pitch. Reich had gotten out of the inning on four pitches. The fans were standing and cheering as she walked off the mound.

Chapter 7

I wanted to see what Reich had on the ball so I got up and sought a seat behind home plate as close to the wire screen as I could get. Invariably some season ticket holder would be a no-show, and I wanted to find that seat before the premium-seat hunters would be scouring all the boxes close to the field.

I found an open seat looking right over the umpire's right shoulder. Once again an usher approached me, and my special pass from Gazzetti shooed her away.

Baltimore scored a run on a walk and a double at the bottom of the inning. Reich now had a one-run cushion. Most pitchers would continue to bear down with such a slight lead. I would see how it might affect Reich's command of the game in the third inning.

I tuned in again briefly to the play-by-play broadcast streaming on the Internet. Holding the smart phone and inserting the ear plugs I picked up Manager Ralston's deep baritone voice talking from the dugout where they had him hooked up to a live feed.

"I'm not surprised really. Oftentimes a pitcher new to the league has an advantage of unfamiliarity the first few outings. But if he has–or she has–any vulnerabilities, word spreads," Ralston said. "The scouts do their job and the pitcher starts having a rougher time of it. Then it's a matter of what adjustments the pitcher will make to compensate."

"Do you plan to pull her at any set time in the game," Smokey Caan asked in his smooth syrupy voice.

"I'm hoping to get five out of her, but we'll play it by ear. If she continues to keep the pitch count down, who knows?"

This was the era that pitchers routinely were pulled after six or seven innings if the pitch count reached 100, no matter how the pitcher was feeling, even if he pleaded to stay in. A complete game, "going the distance" of nine innings was a rarity now. Sixty years ago it was the norm. Relief pitchers, called closers, used to come in to replace the starter in the ninth inning only if he showed signs of tiring or began loading bases with runners.

My opinion at this early juncture was Reich couldn't last in the majors as a starter. There were too many innings and too much time in a game for batters to acclimate and adjust to a pitcher's style. A short reliever only had to be effective for one inning. If Reich followed a strong fastballer, the batters would have a tough time reacting to her speed.

I sensed the fans around me quietly focused on home plate. Looking over the umpire's shoulder at near ground level allowed us to imagine how we would be able to react to each pitch. The view let one appreciate how the batter was seeing the ball come in.

From this vantage point I could see how effective Reich was at distracting the batter with her grand wind-up and delivery, how it looked to a left-handed batter when she spun far around to first base, kicking her right leg high up before swinging back and delivering the ball. It was a flurry of extreme motion and then the ball sailing in low with great spin. She changed speeds on just about every pitch. Her fastball, while not fast when matched against most major league pitchers, was smooth and seemed to sneak up on the batter, particularly if the batter was expecting her usual off-speed pitch.

I watched how her balls came in low and then dipped a little further when reaching the plate, with the effect that the batter too often lunged at the tail end of a swing, hitting weak grounders or slow bouncers to the infielders.

I detected Reich also had a pitch in her arsenal that was still rare in the majors: a screwball rolling off her left hand that turned into the batter. These must have been the pitches that handcuffed Rudy Smith before he lifted a high fly to the outfield. Smith fared no better the second time around. He was always swinging for the right porch and looked like putty in Reich's hands, excuse the cliché. He struck out on three pitches as he lunged and twisted uncomfortably in his swings, the screwball getting him on the last pitch. He strode back to the dugout smiling and cussing under his breath.

There was, of course, another element to Reich's distracting delivery. It was feminine overall even if she didn't throw like a girl. Her delivery would earn praise from great southpaws like Sandy Koufax and Warren Spahn. But she had the physique of a girl, and a shapely one at that. She was petite in size. Her neck was slender. She was flat-chested; but her hips and thighs and posterior gave her all the curves.

Thighs on a woman could arrest my attention from over a hundred feet away. Reich stood sixty feet, six inches from the batter. If the batter liked what he saw one had to wonder how distracted he could become. Seeing Reich's thighs on the street would send a man lusting after her. In the heat of a game I wasn't so sure, but to add fuel to a man's loins was the sliver of flesh she flashed through the slit up her right leg, showcased momentarily as she swung it over toward first base in her wind-up.

I was beginning to lust over her watching her pitch from my seat behind the plate.

It begged the question I thought to pose in the article I would write: Was it fair for a female player to put the power of her sex in play?

Reich rolled on through inning after inning. She looked like she was in great shape and she apparently had energy in reserve. New York had an embarrassing time trying to align their batting rhythms to her speeds. Their bats rarely swung across the same plane the pitch was coming in on. They were throwing the bat out after her low pitches. Occasionally she would come in with a straight hopper (a pitch that sailed upward suddenly) that totally bewildered them.

Adding to her commanding performance so far was the appearance that she was calling many of her pitches herself. She was regularly shaking her head at Morton's signs. A few times he walked to the mound to have words with her. This wasn't uncommon when a catcher and pitcher were new to each other.

As the one-to-nothing game reached the seventh inning, I was sure Ralston would pull her and send in a relief pitcher to finish the game. Not because I saw any wisdom in such a move, but because I rarely saw any wisdom in the major leagues these days.

As it turned out, the game rolled on into the ninth inning and Reich walked out to the mound. By my count she had thrown but seventy pitches, striking out just three batters. The rest of them mostly grounded out. She allowed two singles that skipped through the infield, but subsequent batters grounded into a double play. The last batter hit the ball hard, but on the ground right at Juan Riobonito, the second baseman, who threw him out to end the game.

All her teammates on the field ran up to congratulate Reich as she walked toward the dugout, while the team she defeated stood from their dugout looking out in disbelief that they'd been stymied by this little girl.

Her victory was an achievement without parallel in the world of sports. Not even the weird reality that the Baltimore Baseball Club had no name this far into the season could detract from what she'd done; pitch in a major league game and shutout the New York Yankees.

I called Phil Gazzetti on my cell phone as I stood along with everyone else in the ballpark cheering Greta Reich's achievement. He answered.

"Phil, I'm beginning to think you're a genius," I told him.

"So am I," the rooster crowed, strutting about in his skybox, no doubt.

Chapter 8

Greta Reich had plans to have dinner with some teammates. Some of the boys, as she put it. It was a good sign that she would be accepted. Winning does that. I had called her after the game to congratulate her on the cell number Gazzetti had given me. I asked her if six the next evening would work for her.

"You're on, Frank. What do you look like?"

"Very handsome." I don't why I said it. Her voice had drawn the flirt out of me.

She laughed. "Oooh, I'll look for a handsome man, then."

In the morning, I went down to the hotel café for a cup of coffee and the *Baltimore Sun*. Reich in her wind-up, frozen with her leg starting her high kick, loomed large in the top center of the front page. Headline: WOMAN SHUTS OUT YANKEES AT CAMDEN YARDS. Subhead: Reich breaks gender barrier pitching for nameless team. There was news on the President of the United States congratulating Reich by phone right after the game.

In the lower corner of the front page, there was another item that caught my eye: GIRL'S BUTCHERED PARTS FOUND AT CAMDEN YARDS.

Great, I thought, reading that a psycho had stuffed a waitress's body parts in a black, plastic garbage bag and dropped the bag in a trash bin by the ballpark. But not even that sensational story pulled the paper's focus off Reich.

Monday at noon I met up with a retired sportswriter at the cigar lounge in Federal Hill. There we smoked some fine cigars and talked over old times and how the country was changing. I remembered he had redneck views; but he sat on all his opinions during our smoke, just letting facial expressions and an appropriately timed, "Oh boy," pepper our commentary. One would have to read between the lines to know what we were really meaning to say.

He was definite about one thing. He said it a few times: "I'm sure I could have clobbered her." Most men who had played some baseball in their day probably thought the same thing, knowing how difficult it was to hit a typical major league pitch boring in at 95 miles an hour.

My friend looked at me cockeyed with an amused smile, saying, "The Yankees losing to a dame on the mound with a no-name team behind her– you believe it?"

"It hasn't sunk in yet," I said. The story of why the Baltimore Baseball Club (official name) had no other name was incredible in and of itself. The team owner had caved to pressure from activists who reasoned the old team nickname was somehow an assault on the environment. "You gotta be kidding," I said to myself. There had been a wave of name changes of various institutions all across America. But I didn't miss the old name of this team. I never thought it was fitting for a baseball club.

I knew Reich's legend in time would only grow in a peculiar way with this controversy. Maybe one day her cap with BC embroidered on its crest would be showcased in Cooperstown.

I took a good walk after that, lollygagging around the shops on the Harbor and then returned to the hotel. I needed to shower long and good to get the smoke off my body. I didn't want to wreak at a dinner table with Greta Reich.

At six I took the elevator down to the lobby, looking around to see if I was able to spot her out of uniform. It was a quiet Monday evening. Two people with baggage at their sides were checking in at the front desk. A few men and women were coming in and out of the front entrance or the adjacent lobby. Against the wall was a cushioned bench. A young woman was sitting there in an extremely short dress, her left leg crossed over her right exposing its thigh to the max.

I gazed unsurely about the lobby and turned around back to her. My eyes were drawn fast to her legs, then I noticed she had short, pixie-style blond hair. She was looking at me, smiling.

I smiled back and continued to gaze about the lobby. When my eyes returned to the girl with the legs, her mouth was grinning, her eyes sparkling at me. I walked up to her. "Greta?"

"How could you tell?" she asked.

"Your legs," shot from my mouth.

"Hah!" she guffawed.

She did not seem to be the shy girl Gazzetti made her out to be. We were both smiling flirtatiously, a gray-haired old man and this young hot blonde who was still a teenager. She stood up, all five feet, maybe two or three inches more, and three inches even more with her spiked heels. She stepped up to me and grabbed my right arm with her left hand and we walked out of the lobby with her gripping my bicep.

I led her a block down the street to this Hawaiian fusion restaurant I had often eaten at in the old days covering the team.

Greta ordered a steak, and I a pork shoulder roasted in pineapple. We sat at a booth, sipping red wine. I chided myself for this breach in protocol: I was there to interview her. I told Greta I would record the conversation on my smart phone, which I do not normally do. I preferred to edit in my head during a session while taking notes, but I was already slightly under the influence of the alcohol and the recording wouldn't miss anything. Greta didn't seem to mind.

We were sitting looking at each other across the table between us in our booth when I casually asked her, "Where did you learn to throw a baseball like that?"

"My daddy," she said, touching my heart. She smiled with dreamy eyes and a little girl's expression of nostalgia. She saw me looking into her eyes for more.

"He'd come home from work every day at seven in the evening. We'd go to the backyard. He'd carry out the catcher's mitt he'd bought. He treated me like a real pitcher. He taught me how to pitch."

I smiled tenderly in response to the look on her face. Her face seemed more girlish, more delicate and fragile than a moment ago.

"My daddy was a great pitcher," she went on. "He was signed by the Giants when he was in high school. But he threw out his arm early. He had a chicken arm after that whenever he threw the ball. But you could still see that he had been a great pitcher by the way he wound up and would kick his leg up high when he'd be teaching me how to deliver the ball."

"I guess that explains your high kick," I interrupted. She beamed.

"How often did you play catch or pitch to your father?"

"Just about every day of the year since I was eight years old. We lived in South Carolina. It was always warm. He took me with him to watch the minor league games in Columbia. I go to bed thinking of being with him at the park, hearing him talk about the players, the pitchers. There's nothing better than being at the park watching a game." She paused with her fork and knife cutting into her steak. "It's better than sex," she said with a serious look.

I could only smile. No, she wasn't shy. "What did your father do for work?"

"He was a butcher. Had his own butcher shop before the supermarket took him in. I guess he had been struggling. But even after he went over to the supermarket, every night he would come home with a cut of beef or a chop."

"When did you start playing organized ball?" I asked her.

"Little League. Then Babe Ruth League on the big field. I was the only girl then. After that I had to finagle my way onto the high school team."

"How so?"

"They weren't allowing any girls on boys' teams. Some sports had girl leagues. Not baseball."

"So, what happened?"

"I told the principal I identified as a boy and wanted to try out for the baseball team. The wimp gave in, if you believe it." Her own mouth was open in disbelief at her successful con.

"Do you identify as a boy," I had to ask, given such proclamations were not uncommon today.

"Can't you tell?" she said looking at me with long eyes, taking another sip of wine.

"Hmmm."

"I told my teammates that was all horseshit," she said, liking to use colorful language. "But that's how the school and the papers played it. I didn't care. I made the team and I pitched."

"Is that where you learned to put English on the ball, all those pitches?"

"My daddy taught me to pitch," she said proudly. "My daddy taught me those pitches. We would sit at the table after dinner and he'd hold a baseball and show me how to grip it for a sinker, curveball," she paused while buttering a bread roll, adding, "forkball, slider, the hopper."

"Exactly how do you throw a hopper?" I asked her.

She reached for her purse and pulled a baseball from

it. It had some scuff marks, so I assumed it was the last ball she pitched yesterday, the one Morton handed over when he trotted to the mound to congratulate her.

She held up the ball with two fingers on the hide between the seams, the fingertips raised just off the hide. "The hopper," she said. "Takes a lot of throws to get it right, make it hop."

I was learning more from this little girl about pitching than I had in all my days covering the team.

"I saw a screwball yesterday," I said.

She smiled slyly.

"My daddy would tell me stories about the great pitchers of old, the ones he saw play, like Seaver and Koufax, and the ones from way back he knew somehow. Chief Bender."

"Chief Bender?"

"Some Indian. But he could throw."

"Is your father still alive?"

"He passed when I was fourteen. He came home one night tired, more tired than usual. I asked him how long I could pitch. I was always eager to pitch to him. That's what I said each night when I began winding and throwing. How long could I pitch. 'Pitch till sundown,' he'd say. But that night, I remember, he said only, 'We'll see.'

"He was squatting down taking my pitches and then just keeled over." Greta looked away, recalled that moment. "I ran over and yelled down at him, 'Daddy! Daddy!' But he wasn't responding!" There was no playfulness or flippancy in her tone now. She had tears in her eyes and a lost look on her face. I reached over and put one hand over hers.

She sniffled and smiled, regaining her composure.

"What about your mom?"

"My mom was a dance instructor at the university. She always wanted to see me get serious into dancing. She enrolled me in classes when I was a kid, but when I really got into baseball I begged out of dance classes. With my daddy gone she pressed me again into dance and got me into a summer program at the Juilliard School in Manhattan. It was good, but I missed my daddy greatly and I missed playing ball."

I watched her silently, admiring her grit, and then she hit me with more of her heartache.

"My mom was killed in a car wreck as I was travelling home from Juilliard," she said matter-of-factly, not wanting to draw any pity from me in telling her story. "I sought a job. Secretarial work in the day, waitressing at night at first. Then I went to the supermarket my daddy worked at. He taught me to butcher when he had his own shop."

"How was that?"

"Not much different from being a surgeon. My daddy'd say that. So I butchered for a while."

I tried envisioning her with a cleaver in hand coming down onto a fresh carcass and blood dripping.

"I sold our house," she went on. "But I still had a hankering to play ball. To pitch.

"I started hanging around the minor league park in Columbia. Got to talking to the manager. I told him I wanted to try out for the team. He smiled politely. 'Wait to grow a little taller,' he would say. Finally, I showed up with a mitt and started warming up with the catcher when he was behind the plate waiting for one of the pitchers to take the mound for practice. He took one throw, surprised at how I threw, and I kept throwing. The pitcher had come out and stood by watching me.

"Soon the manager came out. Finally, he said, 'Hey, come to the game this Saturday and help warm up our catcher.' That's how they became familiar with me. Two weeks later a scout showed up, Pete Sake."

"That's his name?"

"Yeah, that's it."

Greta began to eat ferociously. I smiled at what seemed to me to be an incongruous sight: a pretty, petite young woman stuffing her face.

She noticed me watching her.

"So, what kind of relationship did you have with Pete Sake?"

She was shaking more pepper onto her steak. "You think I slept with him to get my shot?"

"Well, I wasn't insinuating anything like that."

"And what if I did," she said. "That's what girls do to get to the top, don't they? And that's what guys do to help girls get to the top, no?" She held up a piece of meat in her fork, tilting her head left and right, then smiling. I was floored by her bluntness.

It brought me to a question I had wanted to ask her, but might not have. "Do you think it's fair play for you to be showing skin on the mound, using your sex to distract the batter?" I asked, grinning in a good-natured way.

"Of course, silly. Again, that's what girls do. That's what pitchers do. They cheat. Spitballs, flashing a little flesh, what's the difference."

"Shouldn't you win or lose by your talent alone?"

Her head sunk down low to the table, her eyes rolled up at me. "Are you a boy scout?" she asked, teasing me.

"Yes," I laughed. "A little."

"Look, if I can distract a batter with my gorgeous thighs or fluttering eyelashes, I'll do it. Anything to get him out."

"You flutter your eyelashes at the batter?" I asked, tongue in cheek.

"Well, at Monk when I'm shaking off a pitch he's calling for," she said.

"You can't get that one by me. I saw you shake off Monk by shaking your head. But hey, you may want to get with Monk on the eyelash strategy."

When her smile seemed genuine, she flashed her humor all over herself. Her eyes became mischievous, her mouth moved with mirth, her skin looked more vibrant. Feeling it was getting a bit too flirtatious, I thought of a good question to ask, relevant to the context of our conversation.

"What did you feel, Greta, when you toed the rubber for the first time to face a man at the plate?"

She leaned into this question, looked brazenly into my eyes, and said, "I felt seductive toeing the rubber." She paused to see if I would nibble at the bait. I kept a straight face.

"I like working a man over from the mound," she added. When she finished speaking, her mouth remained open just enough to show her tongue slide along the inside of her lower lip.

Her candor and lack of modesty was charming me. The serious face she wore now was as alluring as her smiling one. Her eyes scanned mine for reaction. She had me this time and knew it. Then she looked amused at putting me on she was a man-slayer.

"Silly you," she said softly. "Maybe my cunning is feminine. But I don't think I could pitch well feeling girlish on the mound."

Her smartphone sounded some classical music tones. She picked it up off the table, thumbed away at it and put it back down. "You know I was towed into Baltimore? Me and my jalopy. Broke down five miles out."

"Jalopy? That word is a little before your time. Where'd you get that from?"

"I read."

"Oh. What do you read?"

"A little bit of everything."

"Like what."

"Ayn Rand. J.K. Rowling. Sigmund Freud."

"Sigmund Freud?"

"I went to him to find out about my daddy complex."

"A daddy complex?"

"I'm drawn to older men."

"Men as old as me?" I couldn't help but ask.

"Well," she said, with a teasing smile. "You look like a Civil War general."

Soon we were enjoying dessert, cheesecake for her and vanilla ice cream for me. She had but a few bites of the cheesecake. Then she excused herself and was not shy about the reason. "Gotta pee."

I watched her walk away, the dress playing up and down her thighs, the spike heels clicking on the floor. I could not help but think of my ex-wife, who threw on three-inch heels for our nights on the town, and strode like one on stilts. Greta glided across the floor, her feet in pinpoint control of each step like an artist with a brush.

It was hard for me to believe this young woman, a girl really, had just pitched a shutout against the New York Yankees at Camden Yards.

"Oh!" I said, when she returned.

"What?"

"How old are you? Was the program accurate?"

"Nineteen."

"Nineteen," I repeated

"Why, do I sound younger?"

I just looked at her. She sounded a lot older and looked as young as fourteen while her makeup put her in the twenties.

It was nearly ten p.m. I walked my nineteen-year-old date back to the Waterfront Hotel a block away. As we approached the drive to the front door I noticed a tow truck parked on the other side of the drive, a young man leaning against the door. Greta excused herself and walked over to him. They talked for a few seconds and she came back up to me.

"That's my friend. He towed my old heap into Baltimore. We're going to go for a few drinks. Want to come?"

"No," I said. "I'm beat. Have a good time." She put on a disappointed face. I didn't want to be the old man lurking beside this tow truck driver, competing for the attentions of this young girl in a short skirt.

I felt a little deflated, to be honest. She was young, sexy, flirtatious, and beautiful. If I wasn't maturing mentally and wasn't creeping towards old age I would be falling in love with her. All right, I wasn't all that mature mentally and I had fallen a little in love with her. I would try not to let that affect my writing I told myself, taking the elevator up.

I got ready to turn in. I washed my face with a hot rag and brushed my teeth. I looked hard at the mirror. With my full, gray beard I saw the likes of a Civil War general.

Chapter 9

The Nationals were in town for Tuesday and Wednesday night games. The Baseball Club won the first. The team took an Amtrak to New York's Penn Central station on Thursday to get ready for a three-game weekend series with the Yankees. I decided to ride with the team. I was hoping for a chance on the way to chat with Greta and get a feel for how she was acclimating to the team and being now the focus of the media spotlight. The *Baltimore Sun* had pictures of her all week. It started with that telling picture of Greta in her wind-up on the *Sun's* front page the day after the game and continued with several *Sun* writers coloring baseball's new legend. She was interviewed on the TV morning shows. I wrote a feature on her for the *New York Times.*

I walked through three cars and found her sitting in a centrally located coach seat on the aisle. The players must have been parading back and forth past her all the way up to Manhattan just to get a glimpse of her legs. Again, she was showcasing herself in a sleeveless, short summer dress that rode high up her thighs. She looked genuinely happy to see me, or so my ego told me.

Monk Morton was sitting next to her. I extended my hand and we chatted a moment. Greta told him I was on special assignment from the commissioner, perhaps hoping he would give up his seat for me, but he just sat with tight lips.

"Monk, could you get me a coke and peanuts," she said in her sweetest voice.

"You got it," he said and was up, past me and down the aisle toward the café car.

I sat down next to her. I was most curious as to how she was getting along with the team, but I was hesitant to begin that dialogue when several team mates sat within earshot. "How is Monk?" I asked her.

"He's sweet, kinda. A little controlling."

"I noticed you shaking him off a lot on the mound."

"My daddy would tell me the catcher is my consigliere, and I was the Don. I'm not going to pitch against what my own brain tells me."

I smiled and changed the conversation. I talked about what she might be heading into with the media capital of the world.

"By any chance did you see my article in the *New York Times*?" I asked her.

"Yes, I picked up the paper in the hotel. It was a wonderful article. You're a damn good writer."

"Thanks, but I think it might have set the stage for you to be ambushed by a lot of ideologues in the business."

She gave me a quizzical look.

"You're outspoken. That came out in my article. Some of your attitudes may be attacked by journalists, broadcasters, activists, politicians."

"Yeah," she responded. "New York's a cesspool. Let 'em have their swings."

Morton was walking back towards us, peanuts and soda in hand, and soon the train was pulling into Penn Central.

Greta had said let 'em have their swings. The first swing came during a Friday morning talk show of a major network. Greta was being interview by the hostess, Eva Williams, who was going on in a complimentary manner about Greta's trailblazing for women in the major leagues. Then to Greta's apparent surprise, she introduced a third person to join the interview. I groaned when I saw who it was.

Beth Frye walked on stage in a manly business suit and sat in a chair that was pushed onstage during the commercial break to the left of Greta. Her angular, horselike face was marked by a harsh, maroon lipstick.

"I'm sorry," Greta said. "I didn't catch who you represent?"

"Women United Forever," Frye said with a thin smile on her painted lips."

"Oh! Woof! Yes."

"That's W.U.F.," Frye said, sternly correcting Greta.

"I'm sorry, everyone I know calls it 'Woof.' "

Eva Williams jumped in. "Beth, how far will Greta's achievement in the MLB take women in general in pro sports?"

"Well, I think that depends on which direction. I mean which direction does Ms. Reich hope to take women?"

Eva Williams cued her guest to answer, "Greta?"

"Well, if I understand the question, I would say to any young girl what I would say to any man. Do in this world what you think you're big enough to do."

"Well, those sound like great words of wisdom, Greta," said Williams.

"They might be," said Frye, "if her own wise words weren't being sabotaged by other dangerous comments out of her mouth."

"Could you please elaborate," said Greta, as I sat up expecting a cat fight.

"In a *New York Times'* article, you insinuated that women would use any feminine trick they could to get ahead. That's what's expected of them, and they should take advantage it. Attitudes like that will set the women's movement back 100 years. Do you want to correct what you said?"

"No, Frank Barr's article was accurate."

"I see," said Frye, "So your plan to survive in a toxic-male environment is to tease the men with risqué uniforms and short skirts like you have on now, displaying your flesh like, well, like–like a slut!"

"Yes. But not like a slut Woof, like a woman. But you seem more distracted by my legs than the men are."

Beth Frye turned red in the face. Eva Williams tried to come to her rescue.

"I'm sure we're all a bit distracted by such antics, Ms. Reich. You must admit, strippers show off their legs, not baseball players."

Frye looked relieved she was not alone taking on Greta.

Greta's response was to recross her legs, this time her left leg over the right, again revealing flesh high up the thigh to the flank of her rump.

"A pitcher," said Greta, "is like a fisherman. Anything goes to catch the fish. Fake worms. Sonar. Dynamite." Smiling, she added, "Some live bait."

In a matter-of-fact tone, Greta summed up her point, "A pitcher will do anything to get the batter out." Her blonde pixie and oval-shaped head bobbed about as she talked, her posture erect and confidant like a dancer.

"Greta, let me ask you a personal, but relevant, question. May I?" said Frye, taking a new tact, putting a little syrup and understanding into her voice.

"Shoot."

"Is part of this journey into a male dominated sport an exploration of your sexual identity? I'm curious. By any chance, do you identify as male–a boy?"

"Thank you for that, Woof," Greta said, continuing to rile Frye with the soft bark of a well-known acronym. She tilted her head to consider the question.

"I identify as a pitcher."

Frye looked at Greta with disdain.

"Touché," said Williams. "Well, our time is up. It's been a most revealing conversation. We'll take a break and be back with our next guest."

I was amazed as how articulate Greta was, and smart. The nineteen-year-old bested a seasoned political activist, hands down. Unfortunately following such a performance, more daggers would be flying.

I spent the rest of the evening watching the videos of Greta pitching I had taken on my smartphone during the game. I studied her motion. Her grand windup was flawless and consistent. I was amazed that a short female of slight stature could reach the plate and have something still on the ball. I played the game in my younger days.

Sixty-feet, six-inches is a long way to home plate. Many hurlers eventually throw their arms out.

Greta had strong thighs that extended to her rump as one unit. Her legs did not look like separate appendages as many do in female bodies. A pitcher must have strong legs and a strong core. Legs and core are the foundation for the windup and the delivery. Without them, a strong arm isn't enough.

I recalled Greta's arms in her sleeveless shirt that night in the Hawaiian restaurant. She certainly had a slight upper frame, her arms light-skinned and slender. This was hard to reconcile with her ability to throw a baseball to the plate. But I noticed her left arm, the one she threw the ball with, was longer and sinewier than her right arm. This was noticeable when she stood with her arms hanging to here sides. Even her left hand seemed more developed than the other as I watched her eat. She may not have been exaggerating while recounting that she threw to her father every night since she was eight years old up until his death. She had to have developed muscles in her left arm, hand, and fingers that gave them a super strength.

Even at that, most of her pitches dipped at or below the batter's knees. The long distance to the plate worked in her favor in this regard. Either her pitches were losing steam as they approached the plate and falling, or she was in complete control of the ball's spin and speed. I wasn't sure which was the case. She certainly had demonstrated great control during the game of where she wanted the pitch to go at the plate: inside, outside, or down the middle.

I also was distracted by the slit up the side of her leg. I had to smile in admiration of her forthright attitude about the uniform. It made me wonder if she herself had come up with the idea.

Her time in Manhattan attending the Juilliard dance school might have injected some New York manners into her southern charm and drawl. Though I guessed she was probably cussing up a storm long before she got there.

Greta pitched again at Yankee Stadium Saturday night. I was thrilled for her. The park is considered to be the Taj Mahal of ballfields. It evokes a majesty about the game and the crowd that watches, and the men who play. Now there was a Queen on the mound for the first time in the recorded annals of baseball in a big-league game.

She wasn't, however, the first female to pitch to major league players. Jackie Mitchell pitched for the Chattanooga Lookouts minor league club and pitched during an exhibition game, striking out Babe Ruth and Lou Gehrig. The publicity drive surrounding Greta Reich's debut had shook little known gems like this from baseball's tree, adding more color and credibility to Greta's game and to the prospect that she just may be the real deal.

In the second game, everyone was waiting to see if Greta would turn out to be a flash in the pan, knocked out of the box in the first or second inning, and never to pitch another whole inning in her MLB career. She confounded those expectations, however, when she gave up just one run going into the seventh inning. She was pulled by Manager Rallston when she walked her first batter, just the second walk of the game. The fans booed as Greta walked off the mound gazing toward the scoreboard up by the left field mezzanine box seats. The Yankee batters had tried waiting on her pitches patiently the first few innings, but her control was flawless. She struck out six batters and gave up but two hits. Through several innings they were lunging for the ball and swinging way ahead of the pitch arriving. Still, by the seventh inning, Ralston figured she had thrown enough pitches.

Zorro Negrewski stepped up to the plate at the top of ninth with one man on base, waving his bat with one arm at the pitcher, "like the sword of Zorro," wrote one Baltimore sportswriter. Hence his nickname. Negrewski planted a home run into the upper deck in right field to give his team a two-run lead that the Yankees were not able to overcome. Though Greta could not be credited for the win, one New York paper described her pitching performance as being in "a league of her own," playing off the movie title.

But other New York writers were taking her to task for her uniform and her mouth, her comments during the TV interview with Eva Williams and Beth Frye, and a couple of the comments found in my article. She neither appreciated traditions of the game of baseball, the idea of sportsmanship, or the history of the struggle for female equality were some of the charges. I heard more of it when I visited with Phil Gazzetti in his sky box.

"The press has started to turn on her, I can see it," Gazzetti told me forebodingly, as we watched the last two innings together. "Keep an eye out on all the New York papers and commentary from the pundits, CNN, and their ilk. She was being lauded as a hero for girls at the start, and now? Maybe you can help in your reporting. Though that first article! Damn! The things that girl says!" I could hear in his voice he wanted to accuse me of lighting this fire; but he cast any blame towards her as well as those who were castigating her. "They're all assholes. They swarm in like bees. None of them have an independent thought."

I couldn't have put it better. I told Gazzetti I would see what I could do in my articles that would appear in *Times*, *Esquire*, and *Sports Illustrated* magazines the next two weeks. But I told myself I would write what I wanted to write, reflecting what I saw and thought, not anyone's agenda.

Yet Gazzetti was right. These people swarmed in like bees from all quarters. All were responding to the few things she said. One TV interview. They would try and bury her; and if she spoke out again, there was no telling to what length they would go to punish her and ruin her life.

Greta unabashedly kept commenting in New York TV interviews. Her comment on one station, "Girls have pussy power," seemed to travel around the world in one hour. In my day, TV was the land of nice, cuss-free language. Now it seems people flock to the tube to swear and spit out gross words. Greta made another comment, innocently enough, regarding her teammates: "They're a bunch of pussycats." She used the word as akin to sweethearts, but it was taken out of context and treated as an insult to their masculinity. The question put to her was, "How does a young woman stand being surrounded by toxic masculinity in the clubhouse?" It was ironic and shameful that her answer was shaded as an insult to her teammates' manhood.

A New York magazine trashed her for being anti-gay and LBGTQ because she was asked about gay marriage and she responded she believed in marriage between a man and a woman. Another writer for the *Voice* trashed her and MLB for not giving a trans player a tryout.

I thought Greta better get out of New York before she stewed in more controversy.

But things got worse in Boston.

Chapter 10

The team flew into Beantown late Monday morning. Ralston said he would start Greta on Wednesday night against the Red Sox, but changed his mind. He was under pressure of the player's union team rep to give his regular starters more game time. It wasn't sitting well with those men that they were being sidelined for a rookie, and a woman to boot, who hadn't paid her dues.

The team had been faltering the first two months of the season, their pitchers giving lackluster outings. This had given Gazzetti the opening he was looking for to call up Reich. If the move failed it could be chalked up to a stunt to sell seats and shake the team up. I doubted he ever really thought she could cut the mustard.

So, Greta Reich didn't start a game in Boston. But she did star on a morning show that ended up going viral on social media and YouTube which raced across mainstream media headlines across the nation.

When I questioned her afterwards as to why she was putting herself out there so much, she said it was all Gazzetti's doing. His office apparently was acting as her publicist. The more exposure, it was thought early on, the more ticket sales, TV ratings, and fame for Gazzetti. The media was already calling him "the Branch Rickey of our time."

I thought it wise to accompany Greta to the TV station located across from Boston Common. The morning show hostess at KUTV in Boston would lay a trap for Greta with a few questions. The hostess was a pretty, brown-haired woman in her thirties who was simply currying favor with the producer and the rest of the city's liberal elite.

"It's quite a privilege given a shot to be the first female to pitch a major league game. Why do you think a white woman was chosen and not a woman of color?"

I almost cursed aloud, sitting in the studio but twenty feet from the set. Social justice warriorism had spread like a cancer in the media.

Greta's reply: "I don't think there was a choice. There was me."

"That's an interesting perspective. You hail from a state that has a controversial past and present. A state that was flying the confederate flag on the capitol building until recently. Greta, will you right here and now denounce white supremacy?"

As I was watching this my mind fast-forwarded

to how this would all snowball over the next days and weeks into a terrible maelstrom she probably would not survive.

Greta: "Of course. I'll denounce white supremacy, female supremacy, black supremacy, and gay supremacy."

Joyce Withers was speechless for a moment, then finally cut early to a commercial. During the break, she leaned toward Greta and complimented her on her poise, and then her "smart" attire, and then asked if Greta was taking in Boston's attractions. I watched it, wondering how the cobra would strike again.

Back on air, Withers asked Greta, "Do you enjoy being the major league's sex symbol?"

"My sex isn't a symbol. It's at the center off who I am."

"But you're an athlete parading your sexuality."

"I love a parade, don't you?"

Withers couldn't win a point, but the damage had already been done. Greta, though, was jaunty leaving the station. "How'd I do, Frank?" she said, grinning, looking up at me with mischievous innocence.

The fallout from the interview would be radioactive. The headline that afternoon in the *Boston World*: "Reich Compares White Supremacy to Gay Pride," with copy that insinuated that Greta was a robed white supremacist and a homophobic bigot.

Greta wasn't scheduled to pitch and the next game

was at night, so I asked Greta to join me for lunch in Boston's North End at a small hole-in-the-wall that offered up sautéed pasta dishes in fast order. I told her I was working on another article. We sat by the front window as pedestrians walked by. I didn't offer her wine since it was possible Ralston might call her to the mound to relieve a battered pitcher. But Greta ordered herself a glass of red. I said nothing.

Greta sipped the wine as we waited for our plates. "You don't want a glass of red wine?" she asked with innocent eyes. Her eyes could switch from being mischievous to innocent in a flicker of the lashes. I looked at her adoringly. She wore her trademark attire, today a short blue and white pleated skirt with a pink halter top baring her back and belly button. "OK, but for the record, I didn't order you a drink," I emphasized.

"I won't tell anyone that you didn't order the drink. Our secret," she said with great wit. We looked into each other's eyes playfully. "It's my one vice," she said, protruding her lips down toward her glass. "Well, this and sex."

She was smiling widely. The comment had me look sideways toward the cook, a young man with a beard who glanced back and forth toward us, probably to catch as much leg from Greta as visually possible.

"Listen," I said, skipping by her last remark. "I'm a

little worried about you. There's a firestorm created by the media over your outspoken comments. I don't want to see you being hurt."

"A man called last night threatening to kill me," she said nonchalantly.

"What?! And I was referring to your spirits, your mental well-being. Someone threatened you? A phone call, what?" I was alarmed.

"Yes, a call to my room."

"What did he say?"

"'I'm going to kill you.' Then he hung up."

"Did you tell Ralston. Gazzetti?"

"What are they going to do, put an armed guard by my door?"

"Well, something. I'm not sure."

"That's OK. I'm protected with present company.

"Who?"

"Smith and Wesson," she said matter-of-factly.

"You carry?

"My daddy didn't raise a wallflower, Frank."

"No, he did not."

"Look," I told her, "I don't want whatever career you have in baseball to go off the rails prematurely. The longer you last, the more money is in it for you." I was acting like a friend or a father, or something that was way out of bounds, given our ages.

"My daddy didn't raise a fool, either."

"Meaning?"

"My father taught me to be practical. At this juncture, I'll be guaranteed a book and movie deal. Calls have been coming in."

I smiled at her cunning and my naiveté. Reich was no one's patsy.

I asked her a practical pitching question. I was curious how she was prepared for the lineups she faced so far, how she was being prepped.

"Wally," she started, using Morton's formal first name, "and I go over each batter. Tom Insone, the pitching coach, is with us. They go over each batter's weakness and strength at the plate. Like they told me about Rudy Smith's little hitch with his grip on the bat as he starts to swing. That's why I was tying him up with my screwball inside."

"They give you a rap sheet on each batter to study?"

"Yeah, I look at it. It sticks in my mind on a few of the batters. I put trust into Wally's pitch calls for the most part. Sometimes I'll follow my own instincts by how a batter practices his swing and stands at the plate.

"My daddy taught me to look for aggressive batters by their stance and either brush them back or sending them fishing. Laid-back batters might get a ball down the middle of the plate on the first pitch if the scouting report suggest they seldom swing at the first ball. Yeah, I look at it."

She had wrapped her arm around mine, gripping my biceps. Not being sure how the affection was intended, I liked it regardless. Thus, we took the long walk back to the hotel passing through Haymarket Square, stopping here and there to watch the street entertainers.

"Oooh!," she cried out. She walked me over to a side-walk vendor cranking out cotton candy. "Buy me a cotton candy, Frank!"

So, I did. She looked happy, flicking her tongue at the sugary wisps. I wondered if her daddy had taken her to carnivals where this confection abounds. She held the cotton candy cone up, offering me a snatch of the fleeting cotton. I bit at it only to feel, inappropriately, a part of her in some intimate way. When we reached the team's hotel and walked through the lobby we were eyed by Morton, jealously it seemed. Maybe I was projecting my own feelings onto him. Maybe Monk was sending out vibes that simply reflected a catcher's dominion over his pitchers.

Reich saw no action in Boston's Fenway Park, but Ralston told her to keep limber in the bullpen, often warming up with second-string catcher Bill Coleman. Baltimore swept three games from the Red Sox and then flew to Cleveland, the other team that no longer had a nickname because the owners had given in to activists who claimed the Indians appellation was racist against ... well, the Indians: the misnomer that stuck to Native Americans that no one minded except the woke people, the wokies. The wokies believed they were enlightened to all that was wrong in the world: wrongs they thought they could right by revamping the English language. As a writer and lover of the language, I resented any attempt to alter it.

I didn't know what the Cleveland fans were calling their team now.

They could have called them the Cleveland Clobberers because they had seven players on the team who often hit the ball out of the park. Greta started the game on Tuesday night and got clobbered for the first time. The Cleveland Club waited patiently on her slow pitches. She got past the first three innings only because her pitches were stroked hard right at infielders and outfielders. But in the fourth inning the balls started landing in gaps in the field, and the Club scored three runs. Ralston sent her to the showers. I wasn't alarmed. She was knocked out of the box by a good hitting team.

The team flew to Chicago to face the White Sox where Greta got into trouble not on the field but in a department store. The whole incident raised a big red flag. It was triggered by the cover of *Untouchable*, the high end girlie magazine. *Untouchable* had become popular with photo shoots that made men salivate over women seductively clothed. This cover took everyone by surprise. It had both Gazzetti and Commissioner Antonelli calling me, worried that that Greta may do more harm to the game than good if she kept up her outspoken ways and her exhibitionist tendencies.

The *Untouchable* cover featured Greta standing bare chested holding her right hand up inside a baseball mitt to cover her right breast, as small and flat as it likely was, and a baseball in her left hand to cover her left breast. Below, she wore a bikini bottom with the image of a Confederate flag emblazoned on her pubic triangle.

I told Gazzetti, "I thought you told me she was shy."

"Barr, she's got to be warned by someone she trusts. The word is right now, that's you. Talk to her please before I do."

On the other hand Commissioner Antonelli was worried, but ambivalent. "She's great for the game in so many ways but I'm worried she'll be eventually ostracized by most organizations. Keep covering her but see if you can get her to calm it down."

Little did I know that the *Untouchable* feature was initiated by Gazzetti; but she was not supposed to show nudity. This may have been technically accomplished on the cover, and inside pages only showed the flesh of her right leg captured in still shots of her windup on the mound, but the Confederate flag on her panty's pubic triangle was over the top. Everyone came down on Greta for this; but Greta told me it was photoshopped in without her knowledge. MLB quickly sued *Untouchable* in an effort to deflect criticism toward Greta and the league both, and the truth eventually came out.

But the damage was done.

In Chicago's Neiman Marcus department store Greta was ambushed by several dozen black activists, which of course made the news. Store security had to usher her out the back door. To make matters worse, that night she fulfilled another interview obligation. There was a back-and-forth between Greta and the TV show host around her wearing a Confederate flag emblem. But rather than explain it fully Greta only said, "Look, it's not what it seems."

The host peppered her with race-baiting questions and, "Will you here and now denounce the Confederate flag?"

Greta, to everyone's surprise, said, "No, I will not. I have kin that died carrying that flag trying to defend against the invaders from the north. I will never denounce them or what they fought for."

The *Untouchable* cover and Greta's comments created a media storm. News commentators denounced her, all of them wearing expressions of disgust.

Watching one of them on the tube, I couldn't help but shout out, "You sanctimonious stooge!"

The players were split in their support of Greta. One faction had had it with all the undue attention she was mustering, some key starters and a few pitchers among them. Another faction loved her grit. Monk Morton stuck by her, and since he commanded everyone's respect many players outwardly stuck up for her.

Gilbert Rue, the team's center fielder, told me all the players ought to be supportive. "This a historic moment for baseball and for our country," the serious Rue told me when I fished for a comment about her in the clubhouse. "When all is said and done I want her to feel we had her back."

Things had spiraled out of control in the media's narrative of who Greta Reich was. They were not able to trace her German lineage back to any specific Confederate soldier so it was insinuated she was lying. Sometime later I learned there was one Major Gustaf Reich who led a regiment for the Tenth Carolina Infantry; but the media proved time and again it was not about true, investigative journalism in covering the news.

Ralston was ordered by Gazzetti to hide Greta in the bullpen and only call her in if he thought she was the best bet at the moment in relief.

That moment came on Sunday afternoon in White

Sox Park. The game had scored a total of eighteen runs between the two teams and thrown in nine pitchers. Baltimore went ahead by a run in the last inning. The White Sox came to bat in the bottom of the ninth. Baltimore's ace closer, Arny Shelf, was called in. As it turned out, Arny had aggravated tendons in his right shoulder, had felt it warming up, but still came out to pitch. He threw wild and walked three batters. Ralston walked slowly to the mound, looking out to the bullpen. He walked up to Shelf and they had a few words as Arny rubbed his right shoulder. Ralston signaled to the bullpen.

It was Greta Reich walking in from behind the outfield fence. Baltimore had used all its relievers.

Reich took the mound wearing the away uniform, black with purple lettering and purple seams along the slit up her right leg. The flesh of her right thigh leapt out to the eyes as she did her wind-ups.

She struck out the first two batters on just eight pitches. They were too eager to smack her slow balls but she gave nothing good to hit. The last batter, clean-up slugger Sam Wielder, got a piece of Greta's hopper, lifting a fly to the infield to end the game.

Greta's relief outing just may have elongated her career as a major league pitcher.

Chapter 11

There was a brief homestand in Baltimore, and I put up again at the Waterfront Hotel. I ran into Gilbert Rue with his family in the lobby. Rue was from Missouri. He had been traded by the Kansas City Royals to Baltimore at the start of the season and had not yet found a house or moved his family east. He was putting them up for the week, so his wife and two young boys could watch the games and spend some time with him. Rue was a born again Christian, one of a few on the team. After meeting his wife and kids, he pulled me aside.

"Mr. Barr, I hope I didn't give you the impression a few days ago that I didn't take seriously, you know, Greta, showing off in *Untouchable*," he said quite seriously. "I don't think what she did was in God's design. I pray for her. She's really a sweet girl. Word is, Gazzetti put her up to it trying to stir controversy, you know, sell tickets. I just didn't want you to think I take things lightly. I know you're working on a book for the commissioner."

I told Rue I appreciated his thoughts and wished him

good luck at the ballpark. He seemed like a gentle soul. His Midwestern accent gave him a corny appeal with his boyish face. I knew he wasn't all angelic, though, as he'd been caught on camera giving the moon in the back of the team bus one day the first week of the season.

I called Greta on her cell thinking maybe she would join me for a cup of coffee before I had to head off to meet with Pete Sake, the scout who signed Greta. It was ten a.m.

"Hold on, Frank," Greta said on the phone. "Meet me outside the front doors in a minute. I'm pulling in."

So, I was standing out front watching the door man hold open cab doors and car attendants handing keys to hotel guests when Greta turned the corner riding a Harley motorcycle and pulling into the driveway. She wore baby blue, skin-tight shorts down to her knees and her pink halter top, which I could not help but notice showcased her pretty shoulders and fair-skinned back. She flipped up her helmet's face shield.

"Hop on, Frank!" she cried out.

It was a testament to how taken I was by Greta's charms that I straddled the seat right behind her to go for a ride without knowing if she'd had any experience on such a machine. I was generally wary of motorcycles.

"Put your arms around my waist, Frank, and hold on!"

She was so tiny. I didn't feel confident that holding on would amount to much in a mishap. She rode the bike past Little Italy and Fells Point and through East Baltimore. "Where we going?" I shouted. I couldn't make out her shout back.

Soon, much to my dismay, she was turning the bike onto a freeway ramp.

"I don't like freeways!" I shouted, tightening my grip around her.

"Tell me you're ok, or I'll turn back!" she yelled back to me, slowing the bike. But she had already gotten on to the ramp. To turn back would have been a greater risk than the ride on the freeway. I remained silent. She kept on going.

When we were riding on the freeway Greta leaned the bike to the left and slid over to the middle lane. The bike must have been rumbling at 65 mph. She even swung over to the left lane to pass a few cars. I envisioned my head bouncing on the highway pavement in the bike's wake. I leaned forward as she did, looking over her shoulder to the nearest exit sign, hoping she would take it. She didn't.

"Relax, Frank! Enjoy it–we'll be there soon!"

When she finally exited the freeway, she had pulled onto a county road.

"Loosen up, Frank–I can't breathe!"

I loosened my grip on her slightly and she laughed. Next thing I knew she was pulling into a long, paved driveway through a grove of leafy white oaks until coming to a million-dollar log house. She steered away from the house's front porch onto a wide dirt path that took us into the woods surrounding the house. We were riding over mounds of dirt and flying through the air.

"Greta!" I shouted.

She sped on. Then we braced for the worst as a fox raced across the path just ten feet before the bike.

She eased up then and we rode over the course at a slower speed and in a few minutes came around full circle to the front porch. With my heart in my throat, she finally stopped the bike, straddling it with her feet on the ground. She had long legs for a short girl. She pulled off her helmet momentarily, turning her head around to me smiling. Her face was reddened. Her normal skin tone was a light cream color.

"How you like it?"

"Like what?" I said.

"The bike, silly! I just bought it."

A young man in jeans and boots came out to the porch and down to the bike. He looked like a guy who had recently got out of the Army, short haircut, trimmed mustache, lean body with bulging biceps. He nodded to me and said hello, introducing himself as Cory.

"Hey, what kinda juice this baby have?" He had a southern accent, perhaps from Georgia.

Juan Riobonito then stepped out onto the front porch. Riobonito looked over the Harley, nodding his head all the while. "Nice, Greta!"

He stepped down off the porch. Greta stuck her head up and they kissed each other briefly on the lips in a familial way.

"Hello, Mr. Barr, how was the ride?"

"Breathtaking," I said.

"Hey, Greta," Riobonito said, "You gotta take me for a ride on this baby."

I got up to give him my seat. He straddled it and wrapped his arms around her waist. Soon they were off down the trail. I noticed Cory, none too happy, watching them disappear into the woods. He began questioning my relationship with Greta and I told him why I was in Baltimore.

He seemed ill at ease and our conversation was stilted. Greta and her passenger then emerged from the woods to the far right of the property. They rode up to the front porch where Cory and I waited. Juan invited us inside for coffee, but I told him I had a lunch to go to.

"Thanks, baby," Greta said, and they kissed in a friendly way again, as she sat on the bike. "Come on, Frank. I'll take it easy on the way back."

It was apparent Greta had become friendly with at least some of her teammates. Like a father I was happy for her. I knew a team was full of egos. Maybe Greta instinctively knew how to stroke them. Maybe she could keep the team in check behind her.

Chapter 12

The ride back was a little less harrying for me, but not much. I gratefully touched down at the Waterfront and left Greta. I walked through the Inner Harbor, past hotels, ships, and submarines until I reached the cigar club near the Renaissance Hotel. I took the elevator up to the smoking room and found Pete Sake waiting for me. We ordered burgers and cigars and relaxed in the leather chairs.

Sake was a tall, lanky man in his fifties. Unshaven, a blue beard masked his face.

"I read your first book," he boasted. "Couldn't agree with you more. They're all a bunch of spoiled brats. You wrote they don't know baseball tradition and history. Hell, these kids today don't know any history. They don't know when the Civil War was fought, for Christ's sake."

Sake told me he first saw Greta pitch for the Columbia Fireflies, the Class A affiliate minor league team for the Kansas City Royals. He was intrigued by her style and spunk and saw how batters struggle against her slow pitches. The more he studied her the more he noticed the finesse of her deliveries and wide assortment of breaking pitches.

I asked him how it happened that she was called up in short order.

"I could envision her pitching in the big leagues just like she was doing down in Colombia and tying up batters," he said. "I called Gazzetti and told him he ought to get down to Colombia to see her. I told him I'd stake my reputation on her, that she would change the game of baseball. Well, he didn't know, he'd say. Then I reminded him how I first introduced him to the team owner, Farley, whom I roomed with in college.

"Well, he flew down. He was blown away. As he talked about her I could see the wheels grinding. I could tell he was thinking big, just by his comments and questions. Did I think she could finesse her way through a major league order, he asked. I told him it would be interesting to watch. She has a lot of junk on the ball and her speed takes some getting used to."

"I have to ask, was she an exhibitionist back in Colombia?"

"You mean, her legs?" Sake asked. "You know, I seem to remember her in her Fireflies uniform, nothing else. I understand she's dressing to kill up here."

Sake had already poured down two shots of Tennessee whiskey and began slurring his speech. "Yeah, she always had the shape."

"Did you see her game?"

"On my tablet. Couldn't make it up here. I take care of my wife, she's an invalid. I wasn't able to get anyone at the house that weekend. This week my sister was able to come down from Raleigh for me. I understand Antonelli commissioned you to write a book on her."

"Well, I appreciate you coming up," I told him.

"Yeah, she's an artless tease," he referred back to Greta. "That's the word that's filtered down. Some of the guys won't like it, you know. And the wives are sure not going to like it."

Two young men walked into the room past us and to the billiard table.

"How did Baltimore pick her up from the Royals?" I asked, not wishing to join the talk about Greta's legs and her love to show them off.

"She was never on contract with the Royals organization. The Fireflies manager was pitching her on the sly. If the truth ever comes out, he may be a goner."

After we ate we lit up some premium cigars. For me, sadly they filled the void of not having a woman around in my life. Pete Sake threw down more shots of whiskey and we talked over how baseball had changed over the past decades.

Then he said something that stuck sorely with me for a long time.

"You know, Frink," he said, slurring my name, "one day she'll wiss she never flashed tha' pussy 'round."

Chapter 13

The *Untouchable* cover with Greta showcasing the Confederate flag on her bikini panties had more legs than a centipede. The media just wouldn't let it go. Writers, broadcasters, pundits, and politicians attacked her for being a racist, a sexist against her own gender, and a dumb redneck.

Cleveland came in for a three-game series of the no-name clubs, Tuesday through Thursday, Baltimore taking one game and Greta just warming up now and again in the bullpen.

It was that Saturday evening I got a surprise call from Gazzetti saying he wanted me in an emergency meeting.

The Red Sox had come into town for a weekend series. Gazzetti had impulsively told Ralston to start Reich again. The papers announced it Friday morning. Come Saturday afternoon, a protest of thousands of the city's black citizens, joined by hundreds of out of towners, swarmed around the Ball Park at Camden Yards. Death threats on Greta Reich reached Ralston and Gazzetti. The

FBI was called in and a private security detail was put on her.

All this only heightened the media attention and attacks. One little, redneck chick from South Carolina, a traitor to her gender, a Nazi sympathizer, was out to destroy the game of baseball. This was the absurd narrative.

At six o'clock in the evening, an hour before game time, I cabbed to the Park to attend the emergency meeting. There's nothing more unsettling than walking through an enraged mob, maybe an active battlefield in a war zone. As I winded my way through the crowd the faces I saw were tense, many shouting out their anger toward Greta. I was eyed suspiciously. They seemed to trust no one. The looks I got affirmed they had no liking for a white man with a white beard.

Thinking I might trip and fall and then be kicked to hell by the mob for no other reason than being physically vulnerable, I let out a big sigh when security let me onto the Eutaw concourse. I made my way into the ballpark and down the corridor past the clubhouse.

The men were standing outside the manager's office, Gazzetti leaning against wall. When I approached them he said, "We're waiting for Chen."

To explain, Ralston said. "I got my own ring of master keys–in my office." He smiled at the futility of that.

A short and wiry Asian man was walking briskly toward us. The name, Chen, was embroidered in script on his pullover shirt. He smiled at everyone and took from his pocket a large ring of many keys attached by a chain to his belt. He thumbed through the keys, and placed one of them in the door of the manager's office.

While waiting I wondered if the crowd outside was getting further out of control.

Inside Manager Ralston's office Gazzetti and Ralston sat side by side behind the desk. Also grabbing a chair by the desk was Special Agent Murdock of the FBI, and Detective Olden from the Baltimore Police, Downtown Precinct. Zachariah Cole, who was the captain of the force, stood with arms folded leaning against the wall. Kate Bower, the team's media liaison, was the last to show up. She headed straight for the pot of coffee on a table in the back of the room. I got up to get a cup myself. As I poured myself a cup, Kate reached her hand over to me, offering half of a granola bar she had snapped in two. I took it, nodding thanks. We settled into our seats. All of us packed Ralston's office.

The discussion centered around the idea of pulling Reich and designating another pitcher, Ron Murray, to start. All of us to varying degrees thought that this would do little to exacerbate the situation and a couple of us, me included, voiced the opinion that this would be taken as an appeasement and only embolden the mob going forward.

"If you yank her now," I said, "you might as well kiss her career goodbye and set flames to this experiment. Something positive for baseball and for women will have been squashed for no good reason," I said.

"We should all be concerned though for Reich's safety," said Ralston.

Gazzetti looked at Murdoch, Oden, and Cole. "What is our ability, practically speaking, to ensure her safety during tonight's game?"

"If that mob buys game tickets, worst case scenario is they hop the fences and charge her on the mound," said Olden.

"Jesus Christ!" Ralston exclaimed.

"You have to figure some of them are armed," said Murdoch. "Some may find a way to get by the metal detectors."

"We could line the fences down each line with security officers. We could put sharpshooters on the roofs," Olden added. He was a barrel-chested man with a receding hairline who had served in the Marine Corps in Afghanistan. He seemed enthused about the options.

"Great!" said Gazzetti. "I suppose we could bring out the dogs, too!"

Several of us smiled. Murdoch, who was black, did not look amused.

Cole brought some assurance to the meeting. "Look, the chief wants you all to know we have a protocol for handling protests and unruly mobs that's been in place for a while now. After the Gray riots, mayors have learned to let the police do its job. We won't let anything get out of control. If there are protesters inside agitating, they'll be arrested pronto and put in a paddy wagon outside the ballpark."

We all breathed a little easier hearing this.

"Look," said Gazzetti, "Frank is right, there's no mollifying a mob. Best not to show 'em any sign of concern or weakness. We should take measures to be ready though. Have security people put in seats close to the lines so they could hop onto the field in a matter of seconds if need be."

The GM turned his head to his manager. "Ralston, start Reich. No one's going to turn the tide as long as I'm GM of this team."

I thought if all went well, this moment could immortalize Gazzetti in baseball history. I began to realize this was probably why I was brought into the meeting. In my next article and in my book, I could detail the boldness of Gazzetti's leadership to the world. Of course, if all hell broke loose his decisiveness would be criticized as being rash and might cost him his job.

Greta started the game. The protesters in the main

stayed outside the park to act up for the TV cameras. A few of them started parading with protest signs along the aisle above the field level boxes. One sign read, "Yank the white bitch!"

Police collared them all and removed them quickly.

Greta meanwhile was in fine form and got into a rhythm that was beautiful to watch. She would rock back on her right foot, swing far around toward first base, kick that gorgeous leg high, and come across with a throw as fluid as a running brook, the ball spinning, sliding, darting, dropping, mostly eluding the frustrated bats of the Red Sox hitters. Whenever they did hit the ball safely through the infield or on a low liner dropping into the outfield there was always a ground ball double play that followed.

There were plenty of baserunners throughout the game, but only briefly. On one play Reich displayed a move the fans had not seen before when she picked off Izzy Steel at first base. He was leaning and straying too much toward second. At one moment, she had brought the ball to rest on her chest before her windup. Then she bedazzled all eyes by making a quick windmill motion, letting loose with an underhand zip to Zorro Negrewski. His long first baseman's glove lain on the bag with the ball just before Steel was diving into it. The move brought the house down, as they say. The surprised crowd instantly rose up and cheered.

It wasn't until the seventh inning stretch I paid attention to a large group of women in the right field bleachers, holding high a banner that stretched wide, maybe thirty yards. I'd noticed it earlier in the game but didn't focus in on it. Now I borrowed the binoculars of the woman seated beside me. When I read the banner, I cussed softly to myself. There were girls and women of all ages, dressed in jeans, shorts, and tank tops. The banner read, "Go Greta! Daughters of the Confederacy."

Well, I thought, it hadn't sparked a riot so far.

Greta's entire performance was rising above all the controversy for the moment. She went the distance for the second time, giving up eight hits, no runs, and throwing only 85 pitches, averaging nine per inning. I began to think she just might last as a starter after all.

Chapter 14

I sent a box of candy up to Greta Reich's room with a note of congratulations on the win, then drove back north to my third home in the past five years. When my wife walked out on me, the house foreclosed and the dog died, I knew I needed a change. If I hadn't known it, the sheriff would have told me so. I moved out of my Canton row house just days ahead of his padlock.

I moved to Annapolis. I started *Game of Catch* during my one-year stint there, never fully comfortable with the town as beautiful as it was or the people living there. It was me. I wasn't able to mix in with any quarter. I was looking for a city where I could be comfortable living with anonymity. I headed to Philadelphia.

I moved onto a pedestrian street or alley, in Old City, close to historical sites, posh shops and restaurants, and new money. I stayed there two years, finishing my first book and lighting into my second, pretending I fit in among the new-money liberals. It was easy for me to talk their language and agree on many of their viewpoints.

I used to see the American flag as nothing more than a corporate logo for the big companies. I got the liberals' disdain for big business; but I loved America's story of free enterprise and freedom itself. I was never comfortable hearing this country being bashed by anyone.

I had one friend I spoke to in my two years in Old City, a bike shop owner who was a U.S. history buff. I also loved the food and the pedestrian neighborhoods. I did some of my best thinking wandering Philadelphia streets alone. But nothing was pulling my heart there.

After the game on Sunday I drove up to Hoboken, New Jersey, where I'd lived the past year. Not sure if I wanted to stay, I had rented a townhouse a block from the main downtown street that struck me as a small business Utopia. It was the way America used to be in all its towns, offering a diversity of products and services, food markets and restaurants owned and operated by independent entrepreneurs who lived nearby, much like the Main Street I grew up near. Hoboken's bustling Washington Street was wildly successful and because of it, maybe too hip and trendy for me. I longed for a place that was only special because I could call it home. So far there was one pub where the bartender called me by my first name, but no one at the bar I had jawed with more than once. Fact was, I wasn't a talkative person. There was a little Italian trattoria with an open kitchen I frequented where I always got a friendly smile from the cook. I visited the hardware store, a dinosaur these days, and the owner sold me one screw one day as if it were a thousand-dollar order. Yet, I still felt like a visitor. I enjoyed Hoboken; but was keeping my eye out for other cities and towns in other states and regions. I had the money now to be mobile.

That evening I got a call on my cell from Greta. I was in an Italian café eating pasta and drinking a glass of chianti, taking a window table, my favorite perch while eating. The first words out of her mouth were, "How did you know I love chocolate?"

"It was a safe bet."

"Yeah?" She said, a bit of flirt in her feminine, southern drawl.

"Where are you? The front desk says you checked out. I want to come and see you."

"I'm in Hoboken having pasta and drinking red wine."

"That's not fair." Again, a bit of flirt.

"How far is Hoboken from here?" she asked after a moment of silence.

"Three hours, more."

"Can I come tomorrow? I've got the next three days to myself. It's the All-Star break."

My mind was racing back and forth and every which way from Sunday. I was thinking if there was anything

I had to do. I didn't want my silence though to be misinterpreted.

"Frank," she said.

"Yes, Greta."

"I've been raped," she said in a matter-of-fact tone.

"What?" I said, ambushed by her words. "When, what happened? Did you go to the police? Did you tell Ralston?"

"No. I'm not going to the police."

"Who raped you?"

"Frank, can I come see you tonight?"

"You wouldn't get here till ten or eleven. On the bike? I don't think riding up at night is safe."

"Tomorrow morning?"

Her voice sounded like that of a lost little girl.

"I could come down."

"I feel like riding."

I finished dinner and began walking down the street past cafes and shops. I sensed the danger of the streets thinking of my conversation with Greta. I strode round the block and went to my townhouse and turned in. I spent a couple hours tossing and turning before I fell asleep.

Greta called me at nine the next morning from the road to get my address. In about three hours I heard the rumbling, coughing sound of a motor. Looking out the window, I saw Greta getting off her Harley. She was wearing black, skin tight shorts that reached down to her knee with one black sock, one white sock high up the shins. Her white halter top had allowed a lot of sun on her back the ride up. She chained the bike to a tree and carried her helmet up my front steps. I strode to the door to welcome her in.

She was looking around my living room. I asked her if she wanted to take a walk after her long ride up. She turned and looked directly at me.

"Hold me, Frank," she said.

So I held her, pulling her head into my chest, hoping my embrace was making her feel safe. I felt her body heat, her fair skin hot from her long ride under the sun.

As I held her she whispered, "I knew you'd let me come up."

"I'm glad you knew," I said, my chin resting atop her head.

Still in my embrace, she turned up to look at me.

She said, "Pete Sake." I just looked at her. "Pete Sake raped me."

I had a sudden sunken feeling, like something evil was lurking at hand. I had heard it in Sake's voice just a few days earlier talking to him in the cigar lounge when he referred to Greta derogatorily.

"When? Where?" I asked. "I'll go to the police with

you."

"No, I don't need to go to the police."

"Talk to me about it, Greta."

"I'm okay, it happened several weeks ago down in South Carolina. I suppose I was asking for it. Not the first time a man forced himself on me." She started walking away and into the hallway. "Where's the kitchen, Frank? I'm a little hungry."

She walked down the hall in her sneakers and I was struck at how little she was in height. But she was bigger than life with her curves and feminine walk. She moved lightly across the floor like a dancer. Her back was bare, just a tie string round her neck and her back.

We settled around the kitchen table, an old Formica table with silver metal legs. I set up crackers and cheese on a plate and heated water for hot chocolate. She told me about Pete Sake.

"I saw him in the clubhouse Sunday after the game. He was leering at me. He came over to me with his lecherous grin, claiming he'd given me my big break. 'Let's go out on the town tonight, sweetheart,' he said to me. Maybe I was hoping he'd say he was sorry about that night, you know. But that's okay. He'll never get near me again."

I asked Greta to think about what I said about going to the police.

"Frank," she said looking at me with a grown-up's

gaze, not the little-girl eyes, "I just let my guard down. I take responsibility for my actions like my daddy taught me."

"You're not responsible for someone else's actions."

"I like to tease men, Frank. You see it. Sure, I tried to push him off, shouting at him to stop; but then I just gave in and let it happen. Hey, I can be taken pretty easily," she said, eyeing me regretfully. "Maybe it's true, maybe I was feeling I owed him. You know, for getting me my big break. Hey, girls sleep their way up all the time. It's our biological curse or advantage, however you want to look at it."

I tried to mouth some words but wasn't sure what to say.

"Don't look at me like I'm damaged, Frank. I'm not. And if I go to police just to stick it to him, the media will be all over it wanting to make me a victim. That or make me out to be a liar. And you know what I'll tell them, Frank? I'll tell 'em I had it coming. I'll tell 'em I enjoy teasing men. That men are made to seduce.

"I'd tell 'em a man shouldn't be put in prison because a girl's coming on to him and he doesn't have the discipline to hold back. Or he's had too much to drink to hold back. How do you think that's gonna play in the media for me? For the team?"

Like now, she often sounded like an older, sophisticated adult, not a teenager.

I just listened to her with a tender smile, not knowing what I should say. She was tough.

We ate cheese and crackers and drank hot chocolate as the afternoon wore on. Talk changed to the game she pitched, how her teammates were coming around or not to her presence on the team. What they thought about her pitching. Her slight alteration in her uniform. She talked about how she wished her daddy was there to see her pitch.

"All those days he would catch me I would ask him if he thought I was good enough to make the majors. And do you know what he'd say? He'd say, 'Of course you're good enough, you're my daughter.' And do you know what, Frank?" Greta said, wiping tears from her cheek. "I believed him."

She asked if we could order take-out for dinner, she'd pay. I said no, that I'd order from an Italian joint I often ate at down the street. We both ordered pasta and calamari, something she never had before.

As we were walking through the living room toward the front door Greta's attention was snagged by my humidor sitting atop the wide escritoire. There was a famous cigar brand painted on it and a carnival color design. Her diminutive figure walked up to it, opened the lid, and lifted one of the cigars, bringing it to her nose.

I was touched by her curiosity. "Did your Daddy smoke cigars?"

"Mmm hmm," she intoned, her nostrils nearly brushing the cigar, taking in the tobacco fragrance. "Drove my mom bonkers."

She put back the cigar and gently let down the lid to the humidor. We walked together down the street to pick up our Italian meal. Back in the kitchen, she asked if I had wine on hand and I produced a bottle from the pantry.

During the meal, I thought I could be true to the purpose of our association by asking how she felt about her teammates and others in the Baseball Club's organization. She didn't spare her name-calling on the ones she felt were giving her the cold shoulder. But she wouldn't elaborate when I would question further. The left fielder, Hanger, was an A-hole, period. The owner, Ed Farley, was "an old fart," who was younger than me by several years. Others were "pussycats," like Monk Morton and Zorro Negrewski. Second baseman Juan Riobonito and right fielder Elmo Little were "sweethearts."

After we ate, she asked if she could spend the night. I detected a bit of mischief in her eyes, but was unsure about her intention. She said she hadn't packed any clothes. I walked into the bedroom and pulled out a drawer. I handed her a sleeveless guinea t-shirt. "Can you sleep in this?" I asked.

"Of course." She grabbed the white cotton shirt from me.

I walked out of my bedroom and into the den. She was following behind. I removed the leather cushions from the sofa and pulled out its bed. I turned to see her looking at a newspaper clipping showing my mug when I was twenty-seven-year-old taxi driver and was running for mayor of San Francisco, an episode in my life quite uncharacteristic of my aloof nature. A story to be told in my memoir, should I ever write one. She looked over to me exclaiming earnestly, "I would've married you then."

The comment amused me. "Wow, you're handsome," she said, glancing back to the picture.

I came back later to see that she was comfortably settled in the bed. Laying under the sheet she was reading a book by the lamplight in the night stand. I could see it was the book I wrote, *Game of Catch*. I bade her good night.

I glanced at my young face in the newspaper clipping on the wall and walked into the bathroom to wash up before turning in. I looked at my face in the mirror. Aside from the gray beard and the little hair that was left on the top of my head, I looked the same as I always have. I reached into my back pocket and pulled out the wallet and looked at the picture on my driver's license. That guy in a still photo looked like a much older man. Much older.

I got in bed. I grabbed a book of poetry by D.H. Lawrence on the end table and began reading. I found his free verse poems exhilarating, igniting my own thinking. When I grew sleepy, I turned off the lamp and turned over. It was maybe fifteen minutes later that a knock on my bedroom door pulled me out of a doze. The unlatched door was pushed open. By the moonlight showering through the tall windows I made out Greta standing in the doorway, my sleeveless t-shirt falling to her knees.

"Frank?" she called.

"Yes?"

"Could you hold me close to you?"

Her voice was sonorous, sweet, and sensuous in the still of the room.

When I didn't say anything immediately she walked to my side of the bed looking down at me. I looked up at the oval-shaped head and the impish grin I could make out by the soft moonlight shining in. I thought how Sake must be haunting her effort to sleep. I lifted open the sheet for her to slide in. She put her head on my chest and pressed her body against me, her right leg turned over on mine. Her body felt lean, much leaner than I would have expected with the thought of the ample thighs she often exhibited. She was lean and warm against me and we both fell asleep.

Chapter 15

I awoke to sunlight in my window and a barely audible strain of symphonic music – Vivaldi's *Four Seasons*. I was alone in my bed. I propped my head up with my pillow just in time to see Greta flying past the bedroom doorway doing a split in midair like a runner leaping over a hurdle, but with her arms thrown behind her over her shoulders, not forward. I did not hear her land, so light afoot she was and so challenged my hearing these days.

Then she reappeared coming from the other side of the hallway, obviously putting herself on display for me. Her left leg kicking high, and pointing straight to the ceiling in what seemed like a one hundred-eighty-degree motion, so stretched were her pelvic muscles, her thigh, and hamstrings. I noticed her smartphone in her right hand where the music must have been coming from, swinging low to her side. Then back again past the doorway, this time in her spinning pitching motion, kicking high her right leg and falling out of view. She was still wearing my white guinea t-shirt. I quickly envisioned her in a uniformed one-piece dress that clung to her body like the shirt did. Her head then popped into the doorway, her upper body leaning forward ninety degrees, her back arched, back leg out of view presumably raised straight back.

"Are you up?" she asked, seeing me look at her.

We both showered and dressed and went out to find breakfast. I led her into a news shop to buy the paper. There was a magazine rack with about a hundred titles. Greta's image was on the covers of several.

My second article on Greta had put her on *Sports Illustrated's* cover with a picture that captured her in the wind-up. Not that she needed my help getting on a cover. Her penchant for controversy was doing that bidding with mostly articles that were quasi-journalistic and opinion driven. *Vogue* put her on the cover in one of her short dresses; inside was a spread with pictures of models wearing several styles of short dresses and skirts. The headline: "Shortening the Mini-Skirt." I bought both *SI* and *Vogue*, and the *New York Times*, then we walked the street until we came to a good breakfast joint.

At the table, we looked over the magazines. Greta enjoyed looking over the *Vogue* piece, her mouth dropped and smiling as she took in the fashion of the dresses and skirts, and the slender models wearing them.

The *Times* had a front-page article on the Baltimore

protest at Camden Yards that carried over to the sports section. It was fairly factual. But then there was an editorial by one of its columnists that said Greta must go. "Baseball must say good riddance to Reich if it wants to save its sport," was its final line. I didn't share it with Greta.

I did ask her if she was paying any attention to what was being printed and said about her and if she was hurt by any of it. "They're writing and talking about some character they've created. I pay it no mind," she said while flipping the pages of *Vogue*. I found it amazing that someone so young could be so unfazed by these distortions.

We ate a hearty breakfast and slipped back outside to stroll the street. Then we set out for the park along the waterfront where we took a long leisurely walk, Greta holding on to me the whole time. For a good while we sat on a bench and looked at the Manhattan skyline. Down aways, we watched ferries leaving the docks and crossing the currents toward the big city. Greta got talking about all the places in the world she wanted to see, none more than South Africa. I asked her why.

"The music," she said, "the rhythms."

"Cricket is more popular there than baseball," I told her.

'Yeah?" she looked wondrously at me at this tidbit of

information.

"I did a lot of research for *Game of Catch*.

The admission did not deflate her awe of my craft. I could see this in her eyes.

"Cricket batters are accustomed to swinging at the low ball. Hits it off a bounce usually. You'd be rocked in South Africa," I teased.

She put on a crazy face, eyes bulging, tongue sticking out to the side.

"In cricket you'd be a bowler," I added, intent now on confounding her.

Her face comically contorted itself again, tongue wagging out the side of her mouth, nose snarling.

On the way back we stopped at the Hoboken Cobblers, where I picked up my old pair of walking shoes.

When we returned to the townhouse, Greta wanted to see her bike. I opened the garage door, and before I figured out what she was up to she was on the bike in the street beckoning me to get on. Seeing my reluctance, she sweet-talked me once again to straddle the seat behind her, promising to stay off highways and ride slowly.

She took off and in a couple minutes we were moving onto a ferry with the bike, enjoying the noon's warm sun and the spray of the current cut up by the boat.

We docked at Battery Park and I told Greta I wanted to check out the Poets House close by, which I'd never seen. Walking through it, I could tell it would swell the pride of any writer who had written verse, even if just one sonnet. The place, part library, store, and museum, made the statement that poetry was magnificent.

I pulled a book of poems off the shelf by William Kunz, the New York poet this place was dedicated to. As I tried to concentrate on a couple of his poems, I was distracted by Greta taking ballet strides and twirls down the aisle.

"Ever read poetry, Greta?" I asked as she sidled up to me again.

"No," she said with a shrug. "Oh, but I remember one poem from school I like 'bout the fog coming into a harbor on little cat feet."

"Sandburg," I said. She was off again doing a pirouette, drawing an irritated look from a young woman who also had an open book in hand.

Greta's energy seemed dislocated in this setting. On her bike again, we rode through the canyon of Wall Street as people crossed the street from all directions and angles. We motored past the famed statue of the Bull, along the docks of lower Manhattan. My arms tensed and tightened around her as she was on a ramp again, this time to the Brooklyn Bridge. A highway of sorts. Pedestrians moved along on a walkway raised up in the middle. We were travelling at about forty-five miles an hour and I eased my grip around Greta's waist, enjoying the view of Brooklyn ahead and the river below.

When we got off she took a ramp that took us to a street that was below the bridge and we pulled into a lot at a pizza place.

"You know this place?"

"Of course," she said.

We sat down in a small restaurant with pizza makers in view. The pie that came to our table was imperfect, apparently the hallmark of pizza here. Cheese was strewn haphazardly atop the sauce, spices dashed on it the same way. The way the pies were crafted no two pizzas could be alike. It was the way of the world today in America. Uniformity was out. Mismatched socks were in. Untied shoelaces, hats backward. It was a different looking society than the one I grew up in when I would dress in jacket and tie for church.

"How do you know about this place?" I asked.

"Me and my friends from Juilliard found this place. We were always searching for great New York pizza."

"Who were your friends?" I asked her.

"Oh, just some of the girls," she said, offering no more.

Greta had to now seemed like a solitary sort. The activities she chose only needed herself: riding a motorcycle, dancing ballet in a hallway, being alone on a mound.

She liked being physically active and had energy to burn; but on the other hand, she could lose herself in an eight-hundred-page book like *Atlas Shrugged*. I had never heard her talk of friends. She had referenced going out on the town with teammates a couple of times, and she was friendly with the second baseman, and maybe Morton.

I got Greta to promise a slow ride, and we motored back over the bridge into lower Manhattan and back to the ferry.

Once in the townhouse, we laid in my bed and took a nap. I wasn't sure if she was tired or just wanted to lay with me. I needed the nap.

We later ordered another take-out dinner, this time Indian food, a spicy lentil dish with basmati rice, and potato flatbread. After we ate we turned on the All-Star Game. After watching a few innings on my computer in the living room, Greta asked if we could just listen to the game being broadcasted. I said sure and we picked up the game on my smartphone, sitting on my deck off the kitchen.

"My daddy," she said, "used to lay out in a lawn chair in the backyard and listen to a Braves game. I would lay there with him and listen to every pitch."

As we listened to the play by play of the game announcer, Greta went back inside, presumably to the bathroom. She came back and stood before me holding a cigar to her nose. She held a cutter and matches in the other hand.

I took the cutter and matches. "You want me to light you up?" I asked.

"It's for you, silly."

I wasn't in the mood to indulge in a cigar. I told her I would just imagine smoking it and, like her, brought the cigar to my nose, sniffing the wrapped tobacco leaves from time to time.

We listened to the game till the end, the American League team winning in the bottom of the ninth with a home run by Zorro Negrewski, Greta's teammate.

"All right Zorro!" Greta cheered, then telling me the story of how Zorro threw a photographer against a brick wall who had gotten in Greta's face, well not her face actually. He was knelt low and bent lower trying to get a shot up Greta's short skirt. "Zorro," she said once more, "is a pussycat."

I opened the window to a soft air that wafted in, and we changed clothes and slipped in bed, Greta wearing another one of my sleeveless t-shirts. I wore one as well with a pair of boxer shorts.

Moonlight shown through the window, and the pair of gauzy curtains were undulating in the breeze. You could hear crickets from the backyards of the townhouses along the row. Greta nestled her head into my chest once again and I closed my eyes. I could sense her eyes were open.

I fell asleep but awoke awhile later to Greta's restless motions with her legs rubbing against mine. Suddenly I felt her shift farther onto me as I lay on my back, and then she was kissing me. She had sweet, thin lips.

It was a moment sent from heaven as far as I was concerned. I was totally surprised and yet I had expected this might happen. Expected or hoped for it. It had taken all the discipline I could muster the past two days and nights to hold back making any advances or coming onto her in any way. It was an effort to act my age.

Soon she was stroking me and sliding on top, straddling my haunches, reaching back, inserting me into her wet opening. In the moonlight, I could make out her intent look, her labored breathing, and her facial muscles succumbing to the drug of sex.

Chapter 16

I did not expect what had happened that night to last or happen again. I did not expect a nineteen-year old to create a future in her mind with a man old enough to be her father. Alright, her grandfather even. But whatever need I was momentarily fulfilling for her, she was by my side for a third night and once again initiating intimacy. It could only be a matter of time, I braced myself, when the tender affection I would show her would be spurned. In many ways, I still had the heart of a nineteen-year-old myself; but I had lived through many heartbreaks, enough to hold me back.

I was too old to have lasting illusions about anything. Greta's beauty couldn't outshine the insurmountable disparity in our ages. We had lain in my bed in the morning and she had caressed my bearded face, when suddenly she frowned and exclaimed, "They're taking down Bobby Lee!" Referring to the City of Richmond's statue of Confederate General Robert E. Lee.

"Assholes."

The politics aside, I was always flattered when she looked upon me as a Civil War general. Lord knows I didn't deserve the reference. I hadn't fought in any wars.

I almost had.

I had been drafted into the Army, went through boot camp in Fort Knox, Kentucky, and was being flown to Vietnam when I doubled over in the transport plane in severe pain. I was rushed to the base hospital in Saigon. One week into recuperating, the Army Doc told me he was giving me a medical discharge. I felt God was shining down on me.

The Vietnam War had been winding down. Few young men wanted to be deployed there and more so thinking you could be killed and the war end days later. I had drawn a low lottery number and got drafted and became more unlucky to be among the chosen still being sent to the war when troops were being sent home in larger numbers. The situation was psychological torture.

The doc, a smiling, bespectacled young man not much older than me, stood at my bed. "Do soldiers routinely get discharged for an appendix removal?" I had asked him.

"A heart flutter showed up. I'm sending you home."

The only thing surprising about my "heart flutter" was that every soldier doing the Nam tour didn't get it.

On the way back to the plane for the U.S. I saw my

first glimpse of Saigon streets, coolie hats, the Vietnamese riding bikes galore and smoke from food grilling on the curbs. It was the same Saigon I had watched on television back home. That was my tour of duty, I was forever guilty of not serving alongside other soldiers and certainly not deserving of being looked upon as a Vietnam vet, or a Civil War general. I supposed this now was another streak of luck in my war experience. Greta. I wondered how long this illusion of hers would hold up. Was it just the intrigue of a gray beard, or was war that sexy in a young girl's mind?

She biked back down to Maryland to get ready for the team's trip to the West Coast to play San Francisco, Los Angeles, and San Diego, all National League teams. These interleague games began the same year MLB added a third division to each league. With all the interleague and inter-division games being played now, a season in the majors seemed like nothing more than exhibition ball. The pennant drive, once mathematically dynamic and often suspenseful, was now a contrived relic.

I was a little kid introduced to baseball during one of the greatest pennant drives of all time. Four teams were neck-and-neck through the last three days of the season. There were ten teams in the American League and ten in the National League. Each day teams would go up and down in the standings. I was mesmerized. The Dodgers, my favorite team, were in the chase. Philadelphia blew a ten-game lead while the other teams advanced. The Cardinals won the pennant in the last game. My father took me to watch the Yankees play the Cardinals in the World Series. Mickey Mantle clubbed a home run into the right-field stands to win the game. The next season, the Dodgers won the pennant and the World Series. I submerged my days in the games, the players, and the daily standings. Four years later the majors split each league into artificial divisions ... and the pennant drive was never the same.

I had gone over this issue thoroughly in my book, *Game of Catch*, but it still exasperated me, and here I was about to fly to watch an American League team play National League teams.

I grabbed the *Sun* at an airport newsstand. Headlines against Greta bannered several pages. The backlash against her was growing. Many organizations called on Commissioner Antonelli to ban her from the game, as if being outspoken was as serious a transgression as fixing a World Series. One headline really got to me: "Reich Strikes Out Children." A charity foundation claiming to help kids in poverty declared in the article that Reich was making it harder for half of them to pursue the American Dream, by the logic that no business would want to give a young woman an opportunity in the wake of Reich's "toxic entry into major league baseball."

Even an animal-rights organization put out an official declaration that Reich was hurting animals. No reason was given. The country's nut jobs were out in full force.

As the team's private jet flew westward, I read in the paper how one congresswoman was putting forth a resolution in the U.S. House of Representatives to censure Reich for her statements in the media. It was an unprecedented act that would have no consequence even if the resolution passed the House. The House probably would not vote on it, but it served to raise the volume of absurd noise. Headline: "House to Reich: Shut Up." I wondered if Antonelli was feeling any pressure to respond.

I arrived just in time at the airport to get on the jet with the team to San Francisco. I was seated next to team publicist Kate Bower. Greta was seated next to Wally Morton. I passed them walking down the aisle to my seat. She looked tiny next to this barrel of a man. Sitting next to Kate, I wondered who was in charge of the seating arrangements. I wondered if Greta had requested to sit next to Morton.

I got comfortable and turned the *Sun* to the page with the MLB standings. Typical, I thought. In five of the six divisions, the first-place team lead by about ten games or more. Nothing but exhibition baseball, I said to myself, again lamenting the way the game was run today. I was about to comment on it to Kate Bower, but held my tongue. She appeared to be in her forties. She wasn't born yet when baseball had real pennant drives.

Kate, though, turned out to be good company on the six-hour trip to the coast. She wore a long plaid skirt and pale-yellow blouse, had cherub cheeks amply rouged, and was still youthful and pretty, a wide midriff notwithstanding. The thought crossed my mind that sleeping with a nineteen-year-old body, disciplined by ballet and a pitching mound, might have spoiled my taste in mature, attractive women for my remaining days.

Kate was unassuming in conversation as we talked about the ups and downs of my career and hers. Kate had been an English teacher for a small college in Pennsylvania.

"I loved your book on baseball in our culture. But I don't think team owners were crazy about it."

"Go figure," I said.

"I love your writing style, but I have to call you out on a little bit of plagiarism."

"Really? Where was that?"

"No, I'm sorry, in your article in *Sports Illustrated*."

"What was it you think I plagiarized?"

"Your opening line, 'No good deed goes unpunished.'"

"Yes. Is that saying attributed to anyone? What, was

that in one of Shakespeare's plays?"

"No, I don't think so."

"So, who said it?"

"Just about everybody."

"Well, you can't plagiarize a common saying."

"Maybe not, but you can note that the saying is a common wisdom, perhaps."

"So, I should have attributed the line to everyone."

"Yes," she said with a smile and a bit of playful guile in her eyes.

"I think you would have failed me if I was in your class."

"Perhaps."

I learned that Kate got her job as publicist by knowing the GM. They both attended Gettysburg College. She had always been a baseball fan. When she left a long relationship five years ago, she felt she needed a change from the life of academia. She saw a secretarial job wanted for the team front office, and called Gazzetti, thinking maybe he knew of an opening at some club that would call on her writing skills. In fact, he was looking for a new publicist.

"I understand the scout, Pete Sake, went to school with Gazzetti. Did you know him?" I asked her.

"No, not back then. I know of him. He signed Greta Reich. Never met him."

"Um. Yep, he signed Greta."

The flight attendant asked us for our lunch orders. Up in the sky clouds of all puffy shapes were sailing above and below us. "Look at that one," said Kate pointing. "It's shaped like a castle with a drawbridge."

I leaned over her to look out the window.

"Yes, I see it," I said.

"I just thought now of an assignment I should have given my students."

"Describe cloud formations in the sky?"

"Yes."

"Why did you leave your last relationship?"

"We were talking about clouds."

"A good segue, no?"

"Okay. I wanted to have kids. He didn't. My clock was running out."

I just looked at her with an understanding face.

"Years before that, just the opposite. He wanted kids, I wasn't ready."

My mind drifted momentarily to my own failed marriage. I had assumed we would eventually have kids and I would become a father. My wife kept putting the issue off and then her clock ran out. It made me believe that the pill was a curse on humanity.

Lunch was served and conversation shifted to her work with the team. She alluded to the tricky time she was having now with much of the country being in an uproar over Greta, but she didn't go into detail. After lunch, a movie was played. Both of us took out books to read. At some point, I napped and then I got a tap on my shoulder.

It was Wally Morton. "Greta wants to know if you care to sit with her for a while. I can take your seat." He looked at me with a forced patience.

I looked over to Kate Bower. "Excuse me, Kate." She knew I was always looking for more background for the book and articles I was commissioned to write.

I got up and made my way forward and found the aisle seat next to Greta. She had crossed her legs in her short skirt. I thought of covering her with a blanket as she turned toward me while I sat.

She whispered in my ear, "Where've you been, daddy?"

Chapter 17

When we landed I sought out the airport's newsstand. Sure enough, San Francisco papers were after Greta. Front page headline: GRETA GO BACK HOME. Greta had gone ahead to the baggage area. As I was walking to get there my phone's William Tell Overture played. It was Kate Bower.

"You coming? I've got your suit bag here."

I told her I'd be there in a few minutes and noticed I had gotten a call while in the air from Jack Antonelli. I called him.

"Frank! Thanks for getting back so quick. I want you to have lunch tomorrow with a Mr. Lin Pi. Important fellow. I'll text you his cell. When you get settled in he's expecting your call."

"Who is he?"

"He's with the Chinese. Was with the negotiating team. He's in San Francisco to see Reich pitch tomorrow night. In your conversations with him, give him all the positives of Greta pitching for MLB. I gotta go. Give me a call in the morning, your time."

The commissioner had me playing a sleuth, now he wanted me in the role of diplomat.

The Baseball Club and I checked into the Palace Hotel. It was probably too elegant for guests who play in the dirt for a living, forgetting they were multi-millionaires. In the morning, Greta went back to her room, and then met me in the grand dining room, what was once the courtyard of the Palace. There we ate with fine silverware on tablecloths under the highest ceiling I'd ever eaten under. The room was a grand glass atrium with iconic pillars, elaborate ornate toppings, and chandeliers galore. A couple of the Baseball Club players, seated several tables away, noted our presence with their gaze our way. Greta and I looked at each other, Greta smiling coyly. We had been seen together often enough by this time and I was more concerned about the chain holding the chandelier hanging directly overhead than any rumors being kindled.

Greta, as usual, was dressed to attract attention. She wore a scant cream-colored dress barely covering her thighs. I was underdressed for the formality of the room, in a polo shirt and khaki shorts falling below my knees, and sandals. Looking around, others were dressed even more casual. When we broke away from each other after breakfast I thought of the chore I was about to do, wishing I could just lay with this nineteen-year-old girl all day before she'd have to head to the park to pitch.

I had called Antonelli after I had awakened. He clued me in about Lin Pi.

"The Chinese are expressing disappointment over the Reich development. I don't think they want the idea floating in the head of Chinese girls that they too can be playing in the Chinese league. The Chinese men are male chauvinists, regardless of the communist propaganda about the equality of the sexes."

"Do we care what the Chinese government thinks about Greta?" I asked Antonelli.

"We care that they stay on a practical course with MLB. They're practical people, but they're really growling over this. Apparently, they have their own sacred cows attached to their sense of Chinese manhood."

"Okay, so how can I help."

"Did you contact Pi?"

"I had placed a couple calls last night. We haven't connected yet."

"Take Lin Pi to lunch. Talk baseball. Talk how revenues have skyrocketed because of Greta. Tell him it's still a man's game, that Greta's unusual success is her finesse. Hey, wax poetic like you know how. Then take him to the game. Sit in the skybox with him. Make friends. Be the diplomat, for us."

"All right, Jack. I'll do my best."

"You may have to do better than that. We've got four teams scheduled to play in China in four weeks. The games kick off MLB's new relationship with the Chinese. Let me know what you may pick up about the Chinese attitude, their psychology surrounding this whole issue of a woman playing."

When I phoned Lin Pi, a man answered a bit out of breath.

"Yes, the commissioner told me you'd call. I was hoping to be done with my regimentation, but I had to talk long distance with my wife. She's in a lot of discomfort. Close to having a baby. We talked a long time. I'm here in Washington Square. Come meet me here and we'll walk to have a bite to eat."

He spoke with an unmistakable Oriental accent but impeccable English diction. He said he was dressed in black pants and a black t-shirt. I told him I had a full gray beard.

"Like a Civil War general?" he asked, which I found amusing.

"Yes, like a Civil War general."

I walked across Market Street, several blocks through the financial district, up across Broadway with all its signage promoting girly shows, then by restaurants with Italian names.

Washington Square in North Beach was a hangout for women practicing the slow motion martial-art of Tai Chi, young white women sunbathing in tongs, and homeless people lounging or wandering about. People of all ages flung frisbees.

I found Lin Pi. He was dressed in black, standing with legs spread and in a semi-squat position, wielding nunchucks ominously in the air. Then he relaxed and straightened, swinging the two sticks joined by chain about his body like a majorette twirls a baton. He glided back and forth in nimble fashion. He moved swiftly like a young man not yet twenty, though his midsection gave away a man in his forties who loved noodles. When he saw me watching him, he grabbed the nunchucks in one hand and walked towards me, smiling.

"Ah, yes. Robert E. Lee."

He knew at least a slight bit of U.S. history. Given the discipline of the Chinese he probably knew a great deal more than just the name of the most famous Confederate general.

We graciously shook hands.

"Come on," he said, "I know a great place for lunch."

And so, we walked through North Beach, the old Italian neighborhood that was very much infiltrated with Chinese stores. We crossed over Broadway into Chinatown proper and walked a few blocks on Grant Street past several food markets with fresh, slimy fish splayed out on bins and ducks hung on hooks.

"You swing nunchucks like you mean business," I said good naturedly as we walked. "Ever use it for real in self-defense?"

"No need. There is very little crime in China."

He turned into a restaurant that had those intricate Chinese characters–hanzi–stenciled in its window. He led me past a counter where several men were eating. A woman behind the counter nodded to Lin Pi, smiling. Lin Pi kept walking through a doorway, pushing away hanging beads. I followed him down a narrow hallway, down a short stairwell, and turned into a narrow dining hall. There were several Chinese eating and chatting at the far end of a long table. Lin Pi took a seat in the middle of the table and motioned for me to sit opposite him. The walls of the room were gray and bare but for one framed portrait hung behind where Lin Pi sat. I recognized the man as mainland China's supreme leader and head of its communist party. Lin Pi caught me looking up over his shoulder.

"You recognize Chairman Wong?" he asked.

Nodding, I said, "I didn't think Chinese business here looked favorably upon the communist mainland."

"We've helped the owner here with a generous investment, as we have with many establishments here in this city. It's part of our program promoting goodwill abroad."

I smiled and chose not to question the simplicity of this statement.

A short Chinese man entered the room from a swinging door in the room's rear and approached us. He placed a hand on Lin Pi's shoulder and they both smiled speaking in a complex Chinese dialect, I believed to be Cantonese.

Lin Pi ordered for me and soon we were chowing down an excellent meal comprised of duck, eggplant, and rice.

"So, tell me, Frank, what will I see tonight in your new pitcher?"

I was specific in my answer. "You'll see a little girl with a majestic windup throwing a ball at many different speeds. If she's on tonight, you'll see batters struggling to adjust to her pitches."

Pi was quick to get to the point he wanted made. "Our chairman thinks it's unfair to the men who have greater physical capabilities. Isn't she making them lower their game?"

"It depends on your viewpoint. A strikeout is a strikeout. A ground ball is a ground ball regardless of who is pitching it. Greta Reich's work on the mound is all about finesse in delivering the ball and outwitting the batter.

Are you a baseball fan?"

"I prefer American jazz actually, but don't tell anyone."

"If you like jazz you'll find tonight interesting."

"I'm sure I will."

"Let me ask a direct question if I might."

"Yes."

"Are the men in China mostly what we call 'chauvinistic?' "

"In some ways you would say so, but in broad social terms no. Men and women are treated equally in China."

"Is there a woman on your Politburo?"

He did not answer directly. "There are some positions in our society where women excel over men, and vice-versa."

Conversation drifted to my curiosity of Lin Pi's background and upbringing. He related how growing up in China's educational system was an intense and rewarding experience.

"We didn't hang around and play video games like your American youth, or grow addicted to your smartphones."

I wondered and asked, "Did you play baseball growing up?"

"Never. I played ping pong. Very seriously. And some karate, what we call te."

"Your country is having a tough time getting your citizens to catch onto baseball, no?"

"You might say that. But it wasn't always so. Baseball caught on in China in the mid-nineteenth century. It became very popular. Seventy years later your 'God of Baseball,' Babe Ruth, came to play. But the cultural revolution destroyed such sports, charging them to be a decadent import from the West. But since then sports and baseball have had resurgence in China. Chairman Wong is a big fan. And we now have an agreement with the U.S. to integrate American players into our league and also bring your teams here to play. It's a very exciting future."

I found the prospect of bringing America's past time to China an interesting one, with one reservation. The Chinese have a recent history of partnering with foreign governments and corporations in a way that exerts unwanted influence, or control.

"How is your Chairman Wong a fan?" I asked Lin Pi. "Did he play sports in his youth. He's a pretty hefty man now. Does he watch American baseball on TV?"

Pi smiled, following my questions.

"He, too, was a serious ping pong player. But his father had played baseball, and his grandfather, and the pictures he still has of them always intrigued him about the game. Yes, he watches American games on satellite TV."

I remarked that he seemed to know the Chairman well.

"He's my uncle. My mother's brother."

Now I felt I was lunching with some kind of royalty, if a communist one. I looked to the wall again at the portrait of the Chairman. Pi was much younger and thinner. Aside from both looking Chinese I did not detect a familial resemblance.

"Chairman Wong believes that baseball's comeback in China is inevitable," Pi said.

"He sees the game as a finer development of civilized people. Let me ask you a question."

"Yes?"

"Westerners eat their meal with forks and knives. Chinese and the peoples of greater Asia use sticks to eat a meal. Which is the more civilized way of eating?"

"Well," I said, playing the devil's advocate. "On one hand, the fork and knife are an advancement in tool making, giving the common eater greater capability. On the other hand," I said, raising my hand for emphasis, "It takes greater skill to eat a meal of any kind with chopsticks. In that sense, it's the more refined way of eating, even perhaps the most civilized."

"Chairman Wong would agree with you. And he draws a parallel on baseball to chopsticks."

I looked at Pi wanting him to continue.

"I heard my uncle throw out this remark when watching a batter bunt the ball delicately down the line, 'Just like chopsticks!'" Pi was smiling in amusement in recalling this.

"He says the fine art of batting is like the skill of using chops sticks with one's food. He believes it's inevitable the Chinese will master the game of baseball like no other country has." Pi was no longer smiling. I wasn't sure if he was pulling my leg or not but there was some casual logic to what the chairman thought.

Meanwhile I was having a tough time picking up my rice and cuts of duck with my chopsticks. I might have had greater success walking on stilts than manipulating these two sticks in one hand.

The road trip turned into a double disaster no one in the Baseball Club organization saw coming. This evening's game against the Giants had its own certain trouble brewing. I had sensed this ill wind; but the red flag it raised wasn't as alarming at the moment as the one still waving from Greta's *Untouchable* cover and talk show comments.

After leaving Pi in Chinatown I went back to the hotel hoping to see Greta before she left to go to the park, but she didn't answer the phone in her room, nor her cell phone. I rested for a couple hours in my room hoping to hear from her, then took off for the game alone.

I was talking to players in the visitor's clubhouse inside San Francisco's China Basin ball park. I was told Greta's room was down the hallway. As I chatted a little with second baseman Riobonito, I overheard Cliff Hanger, the black left fielder, talking to centerfielder Gilbert Rue as he was stretching into his uniform trousers. "He better keep her in the pen," said Hanger, "because you won't see my black ass hustling for that white ho." Rue was lacing up his cleats next to him. He stood up and put a hand on Hanger's shoulder. "Hey, I can relate."

I was angry and disappointed Rue had not taken issue with the slur on Greta. I should have relayed Hanger's comment to Ralston, but I just pushed it to the back of my mind not wanting to consider what it might portend.

I found Lin Pi in the seat next to mine in the lower first base box Antonelli had reserved for me on my specific request. It was a good angle to watch Greta pitch. I thought in later innings I would see if we could shift to seats behind home plate, another great angle for appreciating how her balls were breaking.

Greta walked out of the dugout taking the mound to boos from the Tuesday night crowd. They say China Basin isn't as windy as old Candlestick Park where the Giants used to play. But the wind that night was whipping around the park. It actually helped Greta, making her pitches more unpredictable than usual, depending on how the wind played on the spinning sphere.

It may have all started when Hanger hit a home run to lead off the third inning and Greta had gone into the clubhouse to pee before he stepped to the plate. He hit the ball over the whole shebang in right field; the scoreboard wall, the bleachers, the concourse behind it, and into San Francisco Bay. Hanger strutted around the bases as the crowd booed. When he crossed home plate and came into the dugout all the players high-fived him or patted his rear, all of them but Greta, who was still in the clubhouse.

In the bottom of the third, Ed Stickman hit a grounder between third and short into the outfield right at Hanger. The ball rolled slowly toward him but Hanger didn't charge it. When it reached him, he got down to one knee as outfielders sometimes still do when fielding a grounder and then lofted the ball to second base. Stickman saw the lackadaisical play and tore around first and kept on going to second. He got in safely, standing.

On the very next pitch, the Giant batter hit a soft line drive up in the air, again, right before Hanger. He could have caught the ball on the fly if he'd run forward to meet it as it was coming down. But he didn't budge an inch from his position and fielded the ball on one bounce. Stickman scored from second.

Monk Morton walked ten paces up the third base

line, standing with his catcher's mitt on one hip, staring out at Hanger. Hanger may have not taken well to being reprimanded by the catcher's body language. The next pitch was hit on the ground sharply just beyond the shortstop's glove extended to the dirt. Hanger could have charged it and cut it off to keep the runner at first. Instead he just stood in a fielder's position, bending down a bit with hands on his knees, watching Gilbert Rue run over from centerfield to field the ball.

Morton now was looking into the dugout appealing to Ralston. At the same time Greta had left the mound and walked past the shortstop to within earshot of Hanger, maybe thirty feet from him. The story I got back from third baseman Jake Fielder was Greta shouting out, "Cliff, think you can move your ass out there!?"

Hanger just remained with his hands on his knees, and when Greta started walking back to the mound, he dropped his glove to the grass and walked off the field. Passing Fielder, he mouthed, "I ain't bustin' for that white ass."

Ralston responded finally by sending Matt McGee out to left field to take Hanger's place. He passed Hanger as he was walking near the mound toward the dugout. Morton was up twenty feet toward the mound watching him.

There was a shouting match between Ralston and

Hanger in the dugout, the players on the bench sitting still as if they were not listening. Ralston shouted, "Are you a professional ball player or a chump on the street!?" so I was told by Morton days later. Hanger shouted back, hands on hips, chest thrust forward, he would not play with "that racist on the mound." He walked down to the middle of the dugout bench and sat. Ralston then walked down and stood before him, was about to say something, but thought better of it. He walked back to his usual post in the dugout corner nearest home plate.

Lin Pi, watching all this, would look at me with a perplexed expression.

Greta was rattled. She gave up two more runs in the inning and two more the next inning before she was pulled. When Ralston sent her to the dugout she walked past everyone without a word, not looking at Hanger and sat at the end of the bench. I'd never seen her angry before. Her face looked grim from this distance where we sat on the first base side.

She had thought she was doing what her daddy always taught her, taking charge of the game out on the mound. She was taking charge when she strode out to confront her left fielder. She didn't think she should have left that for the shortstop or the manager to handle. She was mad.

Lin Pi turned to me and said, "Seems that a girl on a

man's team has inherent problems, Frank."

I didn't say anything to that. What could I say?

When the game ended, I shook Lin Pi's hand. "You must come to China," he said. "We will watch a ball game in Beijing. Chopsticks! But I think it's a man's game."

I left Pi to see if I could find Greta.

There was danger brewing between Morton and Hanger in the clubhouse. I saw them square off and start a cussing war. I waited for it to escalate beyond that.

Hanger at one point turned away from Monk, but then spun quickly with a right-hand punch straight into the catcher's gut. It played out like a cartoon.

Morton stood rock solid, his gut springing Hanger's fist right back to him. He then dove into Morton's midsection, but the catcher just knocked him down as if he were a floating knuckleball. Hanger, a slim, five foot, nine-inch figure, weighing no more than 150 pounds, could not compete with Morton's mass. That and his cleat slipped on a floor more unforgiving than grass.

Greta had quickly gone into her private locker room, an auxiliary training room, and was soon soaking in her private sauna. I wanted to be with her to give her my support but her door was shut.

I stood in the visitor's clubhouse and watched as another player bolted between Hanger and Morton.

That player was the right fielder, Elmo Little. Elmo

had maybe an inch on Hanger. He, too, was lean, and had a gun for a right arm, leading the league in throwing out runners on the bases. His gait was ramrod straight with none of the Hanger swagger. Elmo was a two-tour veteran of the Iraq war, coming out of it waving red, white, and blue. An image of the flag was pasted on his locker. Hanger somehow served but a half year at a home base, coming out of it complaining about "the Mickey Mouse Army ways" and the system in general. When Elmo Little stepped in to prevent blood being shed, Hanger growled, "Uncle Tom, get out the way!"

Elmo clocked him on the jaw right then, sending him over a chair and crashing into a locker. Other players stepped in. Security guards had to be deployed for the next hour until the clubhouse cleared out.

In my hotel room with Greta lying next to me reading a book on Marco Polo, the sailor renown for exploring China, I got a call from the commissioner.

"I watched the game, Frank. I'm afraid to ask how it went with Lin Pi?"

"Good, Jack. Chairman Wong loves baseball and I think there's a path for greater understanding on the present situation," I lied. I didn't want to go any further into it with Greta next to me. "I'll write you a report and give you my thoughts. I want to think it all through first. It was good we met."

Antonelli seemed relieved, said he looked forward to the report and talking to me again.

While I might have bullshitted him, there was an idea cooking in the back of my mind. Convince Wong that MLB only saw a specialized role for women playing with the men; the exceptional female sprinter used as a pinch runner, the unusual feline batter with a good eye and quick reflexes that might one day surface in the game. As far as explaining Greta, she was a rare specimen of pitching finesse and it would be a hundred years before baseball ever saw the likes of her again.

Chapter 18

The headlines next morning: "Left Fielder Refuses to Play for Reich," "Hanger Refuses to Field for White Supremacist," "Confederate Pitcher Torpedoed by Left Fielder," "Baltimore Players Brawl in Clubhouse," and so on across the nation. I read just about all of them from my room at the Palace on my laptop over the Internet. By noon, black and white protesters began gathering on New Montgomery Street across from the hotel. Signs read, "Baltimore Go Home!" "Go Back to Dixie!," "Tar Feather Her White Ass!"

I was astounded at how people got all worked up by nothing more than baseless headlines.

The protest grew tenfold in numbers around the Giants ballpark by five p.m.

SF's mayor called Ralston–at least she told the press she did–advising him not to suit Greta for the night's game. Ralston, a stubborn New Englander, would not be intimidated. Greta suited but stayed in the bull pen.

Hanger was benched indefinitely and when the

press got wind of that, it acted like the old Hearst papers egging on its readers to war against Spain in Cuba.

The headline, though, that got my attention most: "Owners Warn Antonelli." It quoted just one team boss, the hands-on owner of the Milwaukee Brewers, Brick Tarlton. "The commissioner," he said, "better heed what his protégé is doing to the league. If he doesn't send her packing soon, he may be the one who gets yanked." He was a loudmouth who made headlines throughout the season for the sake of strutting his vanity and selling tickets.

Still, I was sure he wasn't the only owner unhappy with baseball's first female player. The press began reporting from anonymous sources that the owners had conferenced with Antonelli over the Internet, and they wanted a resolution of the crisis before it got further out of hand.

I picked up the Chronicle at the hotel's coffee nook and waited in line to pay for it. I thought I knew the man before the cash register paying for his coffee and roll but wasn't sure. He turned and saw me looking at him. He was young and in great physical shape with a trimmed haircut and mustache. He walked away.

Then I thought he was the man I had met briefly at Juan Riobonito's house. My instincts told me he was staying at the hotel and had come out to San Francisco to show support for the Baltimore Club's second baseman. I didn't want to conjecture beyond that if he was the same guy.

Reading the paper in my room, I figured it would be a good idea to take Greta to lunch with Kate Bower. Maybe we could come to an agreement on the direction to take with the media, and pull Greta into that huddle. We might come to a consensus on comportment and messaging without actually having to lay the law down to Greta, a role I did not want to take on.

We took her to North Beach where there was outdoor seating, which turned out to be a mistake.

I thought Greta was understanding the drift of the talk that it would be best to lay low, unseen, and silent for the next few weeks at least. But to Greta this must have seemed like a plan where she would have no control. It went against her nature and tutelage under her father, that a pitcher must control the game.

"Look!," she spoke up at one point. "I'm not gonna play dead. I'm gonna be me."

The problem was that "me" was being characterized as someone other than who she was by the press.

The story being told was that Greta told Hanger to "get his lazy black ass moving."

The papers printed it. The broadcaster quoted it. Thus, it became fact even though it was untrue.

To spice up the hoopla, photos of Greta crossing her fleshy thighs at the outdoor café, began appearing everywhere one looked on the Internet as we dined. Several pictures had been captured by several passersby. I looked at many of them on my smart phone, while sitting across from Greta, like a jealous man watching his lover show herself off to another man. And I wasn't the jealous type. I showed one photo to Kate sitting to my left.

Chapter 19

If all the Internet imagery and incendiary press after the Hanger incident wasn't bad enough, Greta allowed herself to talk to a reporter two days later during warm-ups at Dodger Stadium. Maybe it was the balmy Los Angeles weather or the friendly smile of the female reporter that caused Greta to let her guard down when she should have known better. She should have been on the alert for the ambush.

"Greta, it's an honor to be talking to you," The blond reporter said with her cameraman positioned off to the side. "So far, you've had an amazing run in the majors, though not without controversy. Do you think Cliff Hanger was dogging it in your game in San Francisco?" she asked, thrusting her mic forward, bubbling with a congeniality that contrasted with her line of questioning.

"What did it look like to you?" Greta shot back.

"When you walked out to left field, did you call out he was a lazy black man?"

Greta, now on the alert, just looked at the reporter with disgust. Not giving a direct answer would come back to haunt her in later commentary.

The reporter then changed tact. "Greta, many girls see you as a role model. They say you empower them; your pitching skills, your courage to compete with the men, the uniform revealing your femininity. Did you have any say in the uniform idea, to cut a slit up your pants leg?"

"Well, I'm wearing it."

"You love wearing short skirts too. This seems to be empowering girls of all ages. A survey just out in Fashion magazine shows that hems have shortened by five inches since you came on the scene."

Greta gave no comment.

"Do you feel this is a sign that you are encouraging girls to embrace their sexuality?"

"Ma'am, I'm just here to play baseball."

"Some mothers aren't too happy their daughters are emulating your fashion statements."

"I can understand that, I guess, if I was a mom–which I'm not."

"But what would you tell your daughter if you ever have one?"

"I'd tell her to dress the way that makes her feel good, but beware the consequences."

"What do you mean by that?"

"I mean, if you're going to show flesh, you're gonna arouse a lot of guys and a few of them won't be able to hold back. And don't drink or do drugs. You're really asking for it then."

The reporter waved her right hand in the air. "Whoa! Are you saying the woman shares the blame for a sexual assault on her body?"

Greta twitched her lips thinking about that. "Sure. Look, boys, men, they've all been tamed by civilization. They have to hold back more than girls do. Girls can be as seductive as hell, but a man isn't even allowed to look at a woman before he gets in trouble."

Greta pressed on in her own self-righteous stance.

"I was just reading in the paper–a councilwoman was pressing charges for sexual assault because a man patted her back at a cocktail reception. You believe that?"

"We have laws, Greta."

"Laws? Hey, I don't want to be arrested for parading my legs down the street. Get what I'm saying? I don't think it's right to jail a man for making a move. If hitting on a girl's a crime, how 'bout arresting a girl for baiting a guy to put a move on her?"

The reporter held one hand to her ear, apparently listening to a remote producer in her earpiece while listening to Greta at the same time.

"Hey, these crazy man-haters are trying to castrate men," Greta continued on her roll. "The way I see it, men are animals. They've got natural urges. They can't help it. It's why there's people on this planet."

"So, if you're gonna dress to excite men, then watch out. Is that what you're saying," the reporter asked, feigning bewilderment.

"Yep."

"Wow! That statement flies against the grain of the progress women have made the last fifty years. Women are being raped like never before, girls are being raped on college campuses, and here you are, probably the most famous woman in America right now, telling women it's their fault. Greta, do you have any idea what it's like to be raped?"

"Sure do. Men have forced themselves on me. Some I fought off and some I just relented and enjoyed it. It takes two to tango. I love wearing short dresses even though some men can get over-eager, even though I realize there are some sickos out there. It's my choice. I'd tell young girls to be aware."

"I give you kudos for being candid, Greta," the reporter said, trying to egg her on. "Let me asks you, is it irresponsible to be removing any blame from men in today's rape culture?"

"Men are sweethearts, that's what I see," said Greta,

totally wrapped up in the moment. "I see no rape culture."

I caught the interview on TV walking through Dodger Stadium. It seemed to me that Greta sympathized
with all the young men ogling her, yet she was unfazed
by their lust. Perhaps she saw them as collateral damage
in the war of the sexes, calling for compassion. The real
target of her teasing attire and seductive charms were
older, mature men, I theorized. They were the ones she
dressed to kill.

"Are you saying men should be free to rape women?"
The local TV reporter persisted in what was now a quest
to have Greta hang herself.

"Well, under today's definition of rape, sure. Kissing,
groping, typical male advances, let them go."

"Let them go?"

"The definition of rape today is too broad. It's absurd.
And the women who support it are idiots."

At that moment, someone shouted, "Heads-up!" A
fly ball hit from the batting cage had lofted in the air and
was coming down near Greta. She side-stepped a few
paces and caught the fly ball, then threw it in toward the
batting-practice pitcher.

"Okay, Greta, I think we have enough. Thank you for
your candor."

The reporter must have felt that Greta had just laid

her a golden egg. I knew in watching it that all the social revolutionary, female liberationists would launch a full-scale war against her, on all fronts, big guns blazing. The diamond interview would bring fame to the reporter within minutes ... and she had thrown out not one question about baseball.

Ignoring a firestorm of questions about Greta's controversial views, Ralston announced to the press that Greta would start against the Dodgers on Sunday. I was surprised, and thought Gazzetti may have played a role in this decision. He had flown into L.A. from the east on Thursday, I assumed to keep a closer eye on things after the Hanger revolt.

I had seen Gazzetti at the game on Friday night and couldn't forget his comment to me as we stood in the visiting team's executive skybox, "She needs a daddy who puts a whip to her when she gets out of line."

I heard from the GM again that Sunday morning when the commotion started.

I opened the door to reach down for the Sunday *L.A. Times* when I heard men talking and saw two policemen with two men in suits at the doors near Greta's room. It turned out they were knocking on the door to her room and then opening the door when a hotel security agent approached to let them in.

Five minutes later the William Tell Overture was

sounding on my phone. It was Gazzetti.

"Frank, do you know where Greta Reich is?"

"Why, what's up?" I said, hearing the alarm in his voice.

"Something is up and she's missing right now. Any idea where she is?"

"No idea. She's not in her room?"

"Look, I'll have the FBI wait outside her room. She may show up."

"What's going on, Phil?" I had no idea where Greta was or where she'd been sleeping the past three nights. I had been feeling like a jilted lover, beside myself craving for her attention and her body.

"There's a threat on her life and I'm taking precautions. Don't rattle her with it if you see her. We will let her know when they get her to the ball park."

Before I could ask him to explain, he had hung up.

I called Greta's cell phone and to my surprise she answered.

"Are you okay? Gazzetti has the FBI looking for you."

"The FBI? What a jerk!"

Her animus in that remark threw me. After all, he was the man responsible for her being in the big leagues.

"Where are you?"

"Walking back to the hotel right now."

"Where were you?"

"Why, Frank? I was taking a walk!"

"I'm sorry. Gazzetti called alarmed you weren't in your room. FBI are outside your door right now."

"Jerk!"

"Listen, good luck today," I said and hung up. I wanted to say I missed her these past few nights but thought better of it.

Chapter 20

After she was back and then left with her security escort, I got ready myself. I was uneasy about this threat Gazzetti referred to, hoping it was just a crank call or note. I took a cab out to Chavez Ravine where Dodger Stadium was nestled in between gentle hills and palm trees. I got there two hours before game time. I called Gazzetti and he asked me to come to the visitor's office reserved for the manager.

Ralston was there with a Captain Fratello, a broad shouldered black man with an Italian name.

The captain explained he had brought over a detail of ten uniformed officers and ten more in plain clothes.

"The fans shouldn't notice anything unusual," he said. "The men in blue will stay close to the field seat areas, on the lookout and ready to hop onto the field if someone charges the mound. The others will be constantly casing the entire park for any suspicious activity."

I asked what was the nature of the threat, looking at Fratello, Ralston, and Gazzetti.

"I got a call in my room earlier this morning," Gazzetti said. "It was a female voice, I thought, but thinking back I'm not sure. She said, 'If she's on the mound, bang bang.' And hung up."

"It's probably a crank call from some whacko full of hate," said Fratello. "There usually is no tip-off if there is something planned."

"Unless the person is really deranged," Ralston said.

"We're taking it seriously," said Fratello.

"Why risk putting her on the mound?" I asked, looking somewhat accusingly at Gazzetti.

"If the press gets wind of this, and they will sooner or later," Gazzetti said, "and we've pulled her, it's likely not going to be the last time a controversial player is threatened to cause just this type of reaction. People in public life get threatened, but they try to go on with their normal routines."

Here we are again, I thought, recalling the meeting deciding whether to pull Greta from her start in Camden Yards.

"Look, I'm going to talk with Greta now," Gazzetti said. "If she wants to pass, we and the players will support her. The same if she wants to take the mound."

I left them to go into the visiting team's clubhouse. I assumed Gazzetti and Ralston went to speak with Greta in the room she used to dress. Most teams had some extra room with a portable locker installed just for Greta. Once she had to shower in the manager's bathroom. Once maintenance curtained off a space in the general shower area. Many parks had individual shower stalls. That was how it was with the newly renovated Dodger facilities. When I was in the locker room after the last game it was a curious sight seeing Greta on display making her way past the men, naked but for a towel wrapped around her, seeking out one of those individual shower stalls. She was changing now in the locker room designated for the ball girls, which had a shower stall of its own.

I walked into the clubhouse where the Baltimore players were preparing to get out onto the field. I noticed Elmo Little had taped his American flag onto his locker, and Monk Morton had done the same with an image of a Buddha. The players were loose, with some chatter about facing the Dodger's ace starter.

Before long Gazzetti and Ralston appeared with Greta, suited up. Gazzetti got everyone's attention.

"Listen up. This morning I received a phone call threatening Greta Reich if she took the mound." The room quieted, everyone now craning their necks toward the GM. "It could well be a crank call. But we've taken the precaution of asking L.A. police to beef up security. Twenty officers have been added to tonight's detail, half of them in plain clothes. I want what I've just said to be on the QT. Play dumb to any questions from the media, now, during the game, and after it." He paused, looking around at the faces of the young men in the various stages of suiting up.

"The reason I'm telling you this is because I want you all to be on the alert. Don't be distracted from focusing on the game, but if you're in the field, if some fan is running on the field, tackle him. He may have a weapon, know that."

Gazzetti paused again. The room had grown even more quiet.

"I told Greta of the threat and told her she did not have to take the mound tonight. But we're a team, so I'll ask her before all of you. Greta, it's your call."

All eyes were now on the diminutive, blonde haired girl with the big zero on her jersey, the slit up her right leg trousers. She smiled shyly looking up at the GM standing a few feet away.

"I'm just waiting to start warming up," she said in her clear, feminine voice. "Come on, Monk."

With that, I supposed she might have won over some of the players who were ambivalent about her. She walked out with Morton trailing her.

I thought I would case the stadium, look for any spots where someone could hide a weapon or oneself and then carry out the threat. But what was the threat exactly, I wondered.

"Bang, bang." Someone charging onto the field with a glock? Someone perched high up, unseen somehow, with a rifle? Someone rolling a grenade onto the turf toward the mound? I walked around the stadium inside by all the concessions and the sports bar.

Maybe someone could sit at the bar watching the game on the big screen and use remote control to detonate a fire arm that was fastened inconspicuously to a nosebleed seat and aimed at the mound.

I didn't think it would hurt to let my imagination run wild at possibilities. But I wasn't too creative or original with my thoughts. I began building a scenario where multiple gunmen were perched so that Greta would be caught in a triangular crossfire while in her windup, like many theorized about Kennedy being gunned down in Dallas last century.

But why? That was the question as big as the how. Why would Greta be the target of a conspiracy? Were the worst of the feminists that diabolical? Was there a globalist cabal who found Greta Reich that threatening to the culture it was trying to foster?

I walked around and outside to the park and picnic area beyond centerfield. I looked up and around at the palm trees. I even looked, I'm somewhat embarrassed to say, for a grassy knoll with a fence. I looked wherever It was possible for a figure to be camouflaged enough not to be detected.

While I was in this area, a man in a polo shirt approached me, flashed a badge, and asked to see my driver's license. He asked if I was looking for something. I showed him my license and pulled out my special pass signed by Gazzetti.

I continued walking around, now going to the upper deck. I walked up the highest seats and looked, seeing if I could spot a perch a gunman could use. There were indeed such perches; but the gunman would be out in the open. He would have to be blended in and go unnoticed. With the number of cops here, this was unlikely.

Suddenly a man in casual clothes, sneakers, was running up the steps toward me.

Another cop in plain clothes. He flashed his badge and I flashed my pass. I walked down to the box seats on the first base side right behind the visitor's dugout and found an empty seat just beyond first base.

Greta was winding and tossing to Monk up by the right field foul line. She would look around her and up at the seats between pitches. I figured she could be rattled despite her show of bravery downplaying the threat. I noticed the men in blue in the aisles. Captain Fratello was right, no one today would detect an excessive presence of LA's finest. I then looked for the ones in civilian clothes. They were impossible to spot.

Morton stood up from behind the practice plate and walked to Greta. He was trying to calm her nerves, I thought. He put his hand on her shoulder, then flicked his mitt at her butt and turned back to sit behind the plate to catch more of her warm-up throws.

The Dodgers took the field to start off the first inning. There was a widespread, gentle applause from what seemed like a typical, laid-back LA crowd. Shouts from the fans were not as passionate or cruel as other fans could be. It was a clear sunny day. The Baseball Club went down with the first three batters grounding out. In Yankee Stadium, the fans would be standing and cheering as the pitcher walked off the mound after a triumphant first inning. Here there was polite applause.

Baltimore took the field and Greta walked to the mound. It was that same walk where her hips swiveled a little and her left arm hanging down would turn her left palm outward and inward repeatedly as she took very feminine steps. She may have been a tomboy at one stage growing up, but she was all girl in mannerisms as she moved to the mound, maybe a bit quicker than usual on this afternoon.

She took but five warm up throws, not her customary eight or ten and Morton pegged the ball to Riobonito at second.

The Dodgers lead-off batter walked penguin-like to the plate. His bat was slight. His practice swings were stilted motions with the handle of the bat being thrust toward the pitcher, not the barrel. Greta wound up and delivered the ball low down the middle of the plate and the batter, standing on the right-field side of the plate, laid a bunt down the third base line. Jake Fielder charged in from third, scooped the ball up and in his forward motion side-armed it to Zorro at first ahead of the runner.

Greta was a bit antsy looking often out toward the stands but the Dodgers could not lay much wood on her first pitches. All three batters at the bottom of the first grounded out. I kept scouring the stands as Greta walked into the dugout.

Her teammates went down easily as well and Greta was too soon walking back to the mound. She threw a few warm up throws, Morton threw down to second base and the clean-up hitter for the Dodgers got settled in the batter's box.

Then it happened.

As Greta spun into her grand wind-up swinging her right leg toward first base and beginning to kick the leg up high, there was a distinct, loud crack that sounded in the mild summer air of the afternoon. I looked toward where the sound seemed to come from, between home and third base and I could see a wisp of smoke high in the air and then noticed Morton running to the mound where Greta appeared crumpled to the grass just off it toward first base. Quickly there were a dozen people surrounding Greta, all the infielders, the manager, coaches, trainer, umpires, police.

I froze. I was afraid that the worst had happened.

Then in between those standing around her I saw Greta getting to her feet with the trainer giving her a helping hand.

Someone had thrown a firecracker off the upper deck.

Chapter 21

I was now called, "Daddy," by Greta. She sometimes said it sweetly, but other times affecting a voice of a little girl, no doubt the little girl she was with her father. I wasn't sure from one day to the next which illusion she was holding up: a romantic affection for an older man, or a love for the father she saw in me.

She spent several nights on the road trip in my room. She would knock on the door late at night, a couple hours after the game ended. I would open it and she would throw her arms around me, kissing me on my neck, accompanied by the usual entreaty, "Hold me, Daddy." The first three nights in L.A. she didn't knock on my door and there was no explanation. She had been in my hotel bed three nights in San Francisco, so I was expecting and desiring her during the Dodger stint; but I bore through her absence without a word to her about it. I did not want her to know how much I missed the intimacy between us, how much I desired her.

That Sunday evening after that last game at Dodger Stadium I heard her familiar tap on the door and she came into my room cussing as she walked through the door.

"I looked like a fucking idiot, didn't I! The whole fucking crowd seeing me on the ground like a scared dog. Fucking asshole!" I assumed she was referring to the one who threw the firecracker.

The night she came in after the game in San Francisco, marred by Hanger's refusal to field behind her, she whooshed right by me, her young, irreverent mouth on the loose. "I don't believe that shithead! He should be traded. What, he thinks I'm the KKK?!"

I told her maybe Hanger was miffed when he was congratulated by all his teammates in the dugout after he homered, and she wasn't there.

"What? I had to pee for Christ's sake!" And for an hour she vented, cussing like a prizefighter sitting in the corner of the ring when his manager threw in the towel after examining cuts above the eye. She was angry at being pulled. She had pitched fine until Hanger acted out and allowed Giants to get on base and score. After that night, she seemed to put it behind her.

The following morning our lovemaking had resumed.

On Sunday evening in L.A. the lovemaking resumed minutes after she walked in cussing. There was no mention of where'd she been the past few nights. I held myself back from asking. She got behind me where I was sitting on the bed listening to her rant and vent and suddenly was blowing on my neck and nibbling at my ear. We were going at it soon enough. I swear she was channeling her pent-up fear and anger into sex, and it was amazing.

Each time she came onto me I marveled at how a pretty girl whose world was surrounded by virile men in their prime and in great shape, could keep coming to my room. I was in good shape for an old guy but nothing like her teammates. Eventually it would dawn on me that I kept my emotions in check knowing this was but a fling, and this made me uncomplicated. She didn't fear I'd get carried away.

Greta was the first athlete I ever had in bed. I told myself when I got to heaven I'd have to seek out young female athletes. The muscles she had used in ballet and on the mound, she put to use leveraging this position and that to get into a groove toward orgasm. I had become addicted to her limber, supple body as if her natural balms were imbued with crack cocaine. When I had to spend hours away from her, withdrawal symptoms took over my brain. My mind would recall the texture of her flesh and the scents around the mounds and recesses of her body. I craved the taste of her skin all over, from the pits of her arms to in between her thighs. One time as she lay below me I was lapping under her arms like a hungry canine when she burst out laughing lustfully. "You're tickling me!"

I was a cold turkey walking. I went through the motions of being a writer on assignment with Greta on my mind. Only the aggravating headlines in the papers and the talking heads on TV that were out to get her would pull me out of these lustful thoughts. But it was only a matter of moments when I would again be taken by the craving.

The few nights I spent without her in L.A. had me thinking about my age. I would look in the mirror at the gray beard and war-torn facial lines. I would shake my head. I was no more than an old man with a dirty mind when she was not around.

Half of me was falling in love with her. Probably the nineteen-year-old half that I never kicked. The other half, the decades-old survivor trying to stay young wearing jeans and Converse sneakers, the kind I laced up to play basketball back in the day–that half was jostling for a perspective that could make sense at this late stage in my life. The one my intelligence kept aligning with was that of a mentor who might advise her. There was no future in any other ways of looking at us together.

This was evident to me as we took breakfast together at a café in old San Diego the last day of the road trip. I was reading the *San Diego Union-Tribune*'s sports pages when Greta was fielding a phone call.

"No, I'm not interested," she told the person on the other end." She listened for ten seconds and the said, "I'm just not interested." She listened some more and then said, "Arny, I'm not the ninth inning. You can't close me." She was speaking to Arny Shelf, Baltimore's relief ace.

Sometimes she showed quick wit.

When she finished the call, she looked up at me, noticing I might have listened to her side of the conversation. "You spend a moment with a guy," she said, "and he thinks he owns you."

I just smiled and did not question her. I thought maybe she had slept with the Club's closer, a tall, strapping young man, whom she may have gotten to know in the bullpen.

It was a thought I didn't like.

The last morning in San Diego I looked at her highlighting her face with some light makeup. As she was fingering her earlobes and inserting pearl earrings, I bent down to the nape of her neck with my nose near to her skin. Her eyes looked up at me in the mirror in a way that for the first time I felt like an interloper. I realized right then I had always held back waiting for her to move on me.

I knew that if I did not hold myself back, I could be all

over her, and she would run.

Chapter 22

Back in Baltimore, I was called by Gazzetti to meet with him. The plane arrived from San Diego late the night before and I had settled in a room at the Waterfront. Greta and I left each other alone in our separate rooms. I wasn't sure if she had already started to drift, she was simply as tired as I was, or maybe Arny had worked his way in. But in the morning, she called me, asking me if we could go somewhere for breakfast.

"I have to go see Gazzetti. I'll call you afterwards, maybe Fells Point for lunch."

I met with Gazzetti again in his office. He had breakfast rolls and coffee delivered to his desk. He lifted a coffee cup to his lips, premium coffee one would imagine if noticing the gold cufflinks at his wrist. He got right to the point.

"I want to talk to you about Greta Reich. This is an unprecedented crisis." He paused to reflect on his words and continued, "You've gotten to know her perhaps better than anybody."

"Phil, she's an easy target in the crossfires of the social justice warriors and all the crazy activism in this country now. They and the media have distorted or outright lied about the things she has said to the press."

"At this point," he continued, "I wish it was just all that. Yeah, there're groups in this city organizing boycotts of the Club's games. Like that blackmailing, media-watch mafia threatening our TV advertisers. I can handle all that. Do I cut her? Or do I ride with her? I've been going back and forth on this for weeks. And now, these seem like mild considerations."

"Phil, the girl just won a game for you with a target on her back. She rebounded from the Hanger revolt and got back on the mound after that scare and pitched seven strong innings. All that should count for something, for Christ's sake," I said, letting myself get riled up.

I forced myself to shut up as I glared at him. Then I said, "Well, have you made up your mind yet?" I was ready to launch into a greater defense of Greta.

"The easiest thing to do is say we're sending her back to our team in Columbia to give her time. She'll either die in obscurity, or mature and fight her way back," Gazzetti answered.

"Phil, let's first consider the person we are talking about," I said, trying to be calm. "She's a nineteen-year-old girl who you took a flyer on she might pitch a few good innings here and there and make the team a champion of women and girls around the world–at the very least, boost ratings and sell more tickets. So far, she's turned out to be a wily pitcher. She has great mechanics. Everyone loves watching her pitch. Sure, the jury is still out on whether she'll be a flash in the pan or she'll continue to cut it; but that's so with any rookie."

"Okay, Frank, say I agree with you. It still doesn't alter the fix we're in."

"I haven't finished," I cut in. "You need to look at the person. You got a pitcher who lives and breathes pitching. She got in trouble with the media because you put her out there on all these talk shows. Her *Untouchable* cover created a firestorm because you set her up for it. She hasn't sought all this publicity. Outside of wearing short skirts and a slit up her leg, which I understand was your idea, the only thing Greta is guilty of is liking to tease men and hitters alike so that she has the advantage. Cutting her would not only be unfair to her, the team, and the fans, but to all the girls out there inspired by Greta to make something of themselves in this screwed-up world."

Gazzetti got up and strode to the big window. There his shoes dug in like a hitter inside a batter's box. In apparent conflict he looked out over the ballfield empty of players. Figuring I may have agitated him by pointing blame in his direction, I thought it wise to follow up by stroking his ego.

"You would take the brunt of all the unfairness," I said. "It was you who had the genius to give Greta a try. She's the first female in baseball, for God's sake, Phil. And she hasn't failed, she's succeeded. Which means you've immortalized yourself in the annals of baseball and world history."

I kept going.

"You're going to cut her, Phil? You're going to listen to all the left-wing progressive factions in society tear her down and tear this ball club down? You're going to give up without a fight?"

Gazzetti turned to look at me blankly, and then turned back around to look at the empty playing field. I wasn't sure which field he saw, a field with nothing going on, or a field playing to a full house with Greta on the mound. I still wasn't sure if he was more Veeck or Rickey in his designs; Veeck, thinking the stunt had run its course, or Rickey, ready to double down on his gamble.

"Phil, the money will follow the fans. The fans want Greta. Greta has been great for baseball. Don't give in to the assholes in this country."

After a short while more Gazzetti turned to me and said. "You know, Frank, when I watched her talking to that girl reporter in L.A., I could have just choked the life out of her."

"She's just nineteen, Phil. She'll learn."

"Frank, there's more," he said, pausing and staring at me. "What I'm going to say, I need the utmost confidentiality. No leaks to your press buddies."

He looked at me, waiting for me to give him my word.

"Okay," I said, "What is it?"

"The Chinese government has threatened to pull out of the agreement if Greta suits up for the games in China next month. They're not making their position public. They want to give the commissioner a way to come to a rational conclusion without the pressures that would be put on him if the ultimatum was out in the open."

I let this sink in. I was blindsided by the news but not totally surprised, given Lin Pi's comments during our lunch in San Francisco, and his reaction to the Reich-Hanger conflict.

"She's fond of you," Gazzetti said, a tinge of envy in his voice. "I suppose you treat her respectfully when you're interviewing her."

"I suppose I do," I said.

He walked back behind his desk. "Thanks for your perspective, Frank. We'll see how this shakes out. There's still some time. I've got an appointment coming in ten minutes."

I walked back through the Inner Harbor toward the

Waterfront Hotel wondering if he had decided to give Greta the axe. On the corner of Pratt and Light Streets I noticed the late morning edition of the *Sun*. I bought it to see how much fallout there has been from Hanger's betrayal of his pitcher, and the episode with the firecracker, which the press took off on: if Greta had a target on her back she had only her rotten self to blame, was the line. That's when I saw the headline: BASEBALL CLUB SHIPS HANGER TO LA. Gazzetti, it seemed, had kept this hand close to his vest.

It was the only good news of the bad situation. I scanned the article to see what the front office was saying about it. Kate Bowers would have packaged this. "We had no choice but to find another team willing to take Cliff Hanger," Gazzetti was quoted. "A player must put team above self. Hanger failed his teammates Saturday night against the Giants in San Francisco by refusing to play his position while the ball was in play. Baltimore received a minor league player to be named later." Gazzetti then added this: "Every player must play hard and comport his or her self on and off the field in the best interests of the team."

I wondered if the last statement was a clue of what would happen to Greta. There were certainly sufficient reasons to farming her out without the international intrigue with China. Getting rid of Hanger was a must.

Not doing so would have invited players to act out their grievances, right or wrong, on the field. No sport can thrive without there being integrity of effort and competition on a playing field.

I called Greta.

"What did Gazzetti have to say?" she asked a bit nervously.

"Well," I said, answering the question disingenuously, "Hanger's been traded to the Dodgers."

"No! Get out."

"It's true, It's already in the papers. Hey, I'll meet you in front of the hotel in ten minutes and we'll walk to grab a good fish meal close by."

"Okay, Daddy."

Chapter 23

Sometimes I would lean partly over Greta as she lay in bed and look upon her, my eyes swimming in her adorable features. She had an oval face with big green eyes. Her hair was cut in a short but feminine style. I couldn't imagine any style would not highlight her girlish beauty. I looked upon her this way in the late mornings as we lazily enjoyed the time we shared not having to be at the ballpark. And every time I gazed down upon those green eyes, she'd smile and emit a little laugh.

"What? What are you looking at?"

"I've never seen a face like yours."

"Of course not, silly," she would tease, "I'm from Mars."

I half-believed her, so smitten I had become.

There was no word on Greta's fate other than Ralston calling her into his office to say she may be relegated to the bullpen for the time being. The White Sox and Tigers came into town for the week's games and through Friday, Greta had not seen action.

Saturday morning, she woke me by straddling my hips before cantering on her mount for a blissful ride, again channeling her anxiety into sex. When she reached her destination by my holding steady, she folded on my stomach and chest and soon her breathing softened and her heart let up its pace.

Her head still on my chest, she said, "I feel like they're going to send me to some cornfield league."

"Hey, even if they did that, the cornfields may be better for your mental health than all these attacks on you."

"I thought you were on my side, Daddy," she said, righting her face to look at me.

"I am on your side."

"Are you sure?" she asked, wide-eyed, kissing my lips.

"As sure as that kiss."

But she looked at me, biting her lip. I knew then, if I told her about the Chinese she would be devastated.

When she came out from her shower, wearing a white robe provided by the hotel, she was toweling her hair, asking, "You think I'll still be with the Club after this week?"

"Think positive," was all I could say.

"He's going to exile me," she said with certainty in her tone. Then she added, "Like Napoleon to Elba Island. Or worse, to St. Helena, where the women libbers will make sure I die."

The media portrayed Greta as an ignorant, young redneck. There was a little truth in that; however, she amazed me now and then with small nuggets of history she had read from a book or off the Internet. She was a jock above all, super-dedicated to pitching a baseball. But she also had a constant curiosity that drove her to learn new things.

"Maybe all this bullshit will blow over as we get closer to the trip to China. The media will be focused on that."

"Maybe," I said.

After I showered she told me she was going to go in the early afternoon to the clubhouse to dip into her private sauna and clear her head. She would then have the trainer work on her left arm and shoulder she felt had been stressed during her last outing. She said she had spoken to Gazzetti and he encouraged her to go in. "Maybe I'll point-blank ask him," she remarked, changing into one of her short dresses.

Meanwhile I got a call from Kate Bower.

"There's a poetry festival at Paterson Park this afternoon. You interested?"

I told Kate I would look for her there at about two o'clock. Then I asked Greta if she'd be interested in coming along.

"No, I'll stick with my plans, you go. You're a writer,

you must like those things."

I was hoping for a sign of jealousy but there was none. We kissed before she left my room and I left awhile later taking the long walk to Paterson Park.

It was an overcast day without the threat of rain. There were two sizable white tents staked on a large field. I called Kate and we met up at a hot dog stand located near one of the tents.

"Wanna hot dog?" Asked Kate. "I'll buy."

"I was looking forward to a non-baseball experience," I said.

"Yeah, so was I."

"But I'll have a dog, just mustard."

We ate standing while surveying the neighborhood across from the park grounds.

"Thanks for inviting me, Kate."

"Any time. You were the first person that popped in my mind when I saw an article on the festival."

We walked into one of the tents. There was seating for about 100 people and a small stage with a podium and mike. Most of the seats were filled with men and women of all ages. There was a woman reading her poetry at the mike, so we sat and listened.

A lot of the poetry were gripes against the greed of corporate America. Other poets were ranting against so-called "toxic masculinity" and the evil "patriarchy." But there was one poet whose verse were impressions about Baltimore's streets that I found evocative, having called Baltimore my home for many years. All of the readers were interesting for one reason or another regardless of their writing talent. It was a sign I needed this break from covering Greta in the big leagues and the media hurricane that had followed.

"I should have brought some of my poetry," Kate said.

"Yes, you should have. Email me some if you can."

"Hmm," she said.

Then her phone rang with what struck me as cryptic organ music.

Kate put the phone to her ear and then her mouth dropped. "No!" she cried out. She walked out of the tent with the phone to her ear and me on her heels.

I looked at her waiting for her to tell me what it was.

She had a look of horror on her face, her lower lip and the cleft of her chin drawn in. She first tried to speak when her mouth dropped open but nothing came out. Finally, with a halting voice:

"Greta Reich—has been found in the clubhouse—dead. He says she drowned in her sauna."

I put my hand to cover half my face. When I felt my facial muscles still intact I dropped my hand and looked at Kate with disbelief, feeling a slow, silent, mushrooming explosion of despair. What was around me began to overwhelm my sense of the ground beneath my feet. All purpose was sucked out of the air. I staggered, my legs weakened all of a sudden, and dropped to the grass. It was clear as day to me now I had fallen for her as hard as a big, steel safe falls from a tall building.

"Kate, who told you this?" I asked looking up from where I sat, arms hanging over my knees. I tried to hope it was a prank.

"That was my contact, Chen, in stadium security. We'd better get over there."

I got to my feet, feeling punched in the gut. I thought, this couldn't be. I thought of my last moments with her in the room. I thought that if I'd only convinced her to take a break and go to the festival with me…

Kate hooked my arm and led me down to the sidewalk and we walked to her car parked two blocks away.

Chapter 24

The funeral took place on a hill with a view of Camden Yards. The Baseball Club had attendance restricted to team members and staff. A reporter from the *Sun* and the *Reporter* was allowed, but no media cameras. The services were not publicized, as Gazzetti wanted to avoid any protests. Greta had no family who attended; if she did have any cousins, aunts or uncles, none came. Commissioner Antonelli spoke at the gravesite as the Monday morning sun shone through a light mist. Most team members wore a tie with short sleeve dress shirts. A few of the Hispanic players wore guayaberas hanging by their hips. The temperature was a warm eighty-five degrees with high humidity.

"Everyone here today will remember the young woman who lit up the imagination of men and women around the world," the commissioner spoke to the small crowd. "Her teammates may recall her as some kind of comet that struck Camden Yards on June tenth last month, when Greta became the first woman to play major league baseball, pitching a shutout against the mighty New York Yankees."

I looked at Wally Morton, who had caught Greta in that game. His lips were tightened and I thought I detected pride swelling his chest.

"We will never know how long Greta would have continued to baffle opposing batters. We only know that when she stepped onto the mound she pitched to win, and did win. And in winning, won the respect of her teammates and all America. As the first woman to play in the big leagues, she inspired women and girls of all ages, while earning the admiration of the men who play baseball."

I was impressed that Antonelli's address was delivered without notes or script of any kind. Maybe he memorized it.

"It is said only the good die young. Greta Reich now belongs to the ages and the folklore of baseball legend. We salute you, Greta. May God shine eternal light on you. May you now rest in peace."

It was that last line where anyone might infer that Greta had been a troubled soul, inferring so only because the media had run with the story that she had drowned herself. A vile narrative it was: the media spotlight and all the enmity that had suddenly swirled around her, had been so overwhelming that she had taken her own life.

When Kate Bower and I had arrived at the team's clubhouse, police had already cordoned off the area as a crime scene. Greta, we were told, had eventually been lifted out of the sauna tub and lain atop a massage table and covered. The coroner had been examining her a good while before he gave the nod to get her out to the morgue. He was still inside by the time we got there. These sparse details were filtered to Kate by her security contact standing in the corridor off Greta's private locker room. We were not allowed in.

There was a rush to do an autopsy that afternoon and evening. On Sunday, Gazzetti had the body put in a casket and carried to the infield behind the mound for the seventh inning stretch. The pall bearers stood away from the casket, the Baseball Club and White Sox players stood before their dugouts with hats on their chests. On the big screen in centerfield, a video showing Greta pitching played to the traditional song: "Take Me Out to the Ball Game." I was still too shocked to release tears, but everyone else at the game made up for my dry cheeks. Watching Greta with her grand windup on the mound with that song playing brought goosebumps and my heart warmed in admiration at what she had accomplished against all odds. I watched like any fan did.

After the small graveside service on Monday, I skipped the wake taking place at Bambino's bar in Camden Yards, not wanting to shed or hide my loss, and drove back north to my flat in Hoboken. I had finally gotten used to living alone after the divorce. Now the space of the flat with only me in it, was no longer any comfort. Greta had spent just three nights here, and other nights in hotels with me. It was only a short stretch of a couple weeks, but it seemed like we'd been lovers for a long time.

I was not able to write any articles, or start work at all on my book about Greta's time with the Baseball Club. Esquire was expecting 2,000 words by week's end. I moped about my townhouse, pacing like a sad, caged beast. I spent restless nights thinking about her. Too beautiful she was for too short a time. I remembered watching my very first fireworks sitting on the roof of the family car with my sister and then coming home to bed, the burst of stars playing in my head much of the night. That's how Greta's emergence and departure from my life was playing in my head now.

I don't think I spent a more tortuous weekend. My wife walking out on me was tough, as were those empty rooms then; but there was a history and complexity of that relationship that served as crevices in the cliff I found myself clinging to. Now I felt I was in a free fall.

I had met Greta when I was engrossed in my new life as an independent writer. These days had filled my mind with creative projects, some that were in progress.

The most basic animal in my soul was hibernating as my awareness of life tried to reason with the inevitable: that I was now on the downward slope of my existence. I had held back hoping to love again. That merry-go-round it seemed to me was now for the young.

Then before I could understand exactly what was happening, a young, beautiful girl wanted to lay by my side and love me. I realized only after she was gone that she had resurrected my manhood and the will to live again with all my appetites.

The following Tuesday, I was driving through the Lincoln Tunnel to midtown Manhattan and Park Avenue for my second meeting with the commissioner. He had called me the day before saying he wanted to revise the assignment he had given me two months ago. Without any enthusiasm, I agreed to meet at his office. I was not able to contemplate the book I was commissioned to write since her death.

The usual drab surroundings of the drive through the Lincoln Tunnel into Manhattan was accented by a dreary overcast morning, drizzling rain, and heavy air. From leaving my air-conditioned car to walking around the block to MLB's doors on Park Avenue I had already started to sweat.

Antonelli's office was so air conditioned that I felt cold on my bare arms as he rocked back and forth in the leather chair behind his desk.

"We both would have looked forward to this meeting with some excitement. Greta's passing, though?" Antonelli, said, shaking his head, not finishing the sentence that could only end in deep sadness.

"Have you seen the stories in the media that have followed her death?" he asked me, pointedly.

"Maybe some," I said. "I haven't been up and at 'em much these days to scan news as I normally do."

"The same scumbags! Their lies and smears are still there. But not as overt. More subtle now," Anotnelli said. "They've changed their agenda. Now that their devil is dead, they've decided to claim her achievements for their own causes. But she had what was coming to her, they say. She was still the racist, homophobic, sexist tart, but a talented one who proved that women could compete with men on any playing field. She was too immature, they say, to handle the consequences of her irresponsible and hateful ways.

"So even after she's been buried, they still excoriate her," he said, expressing his disgust.

I looked at him, tired of all the shit that led up to her death.

"They're all happy with the suicide. They're pushing that narrative like they pushed the others."

I was wondering what this all was leading to?

"Frank, do you believe Greta killed herself? You came to know her."

"Well, the coroner's report coincides with suicide. I don't really know the details."

"Frank, the coroner's report was inconclusive. There's some mystery about how she drowned."

"Well, I know she couldn't swim."

"How do you know that? Is it relevant? In a tub?"

I dodged the question. Greta and I had spent some time one morning in the hotel pool where she would cling to me, wrapping her arms and legs around my body. She told me she couldn't swim. This didn't seem credible to me, given her athletic prowess; but I liked when she wrapped herself around me.

"Frank, no one can swim in a tub."

"If you're asking me if I thought she was the kind of person who could, or would, kill herself? I'd say no," I finally answered. "She was a fighter. All the attacks that would have gotten anybody down ... she didn't let them get to her. After Hanger, she was worried Gazzetti might farm her off; but she was still Greta, eager to pitch."

"Frank, there's no way in hell that girl committed suicide. To the very end she was able to control the most cherished part of her life. The pitching mound. She had just made major league history. And she was no wallflower."

"No," I chimed in, remembering her own words, "She was no wallflower."

"Frank, I'll be damned if we're going to let the bastards keep Greta in a suicide's grave. I am altering your assignment."

I looked at him with puzzled eyes.

"You're going back to Baltimore to continue getting background on Greta for the book. You will continue to interview the players and whoever else gives you cause. But now you have a dual purpose. One is to write an objective book, and two, to investigate into the murder of Greta Reich, with the book as a cover."

"You want me to investigate a murder?" I was flabbergasted.

"The people you question won't suspect it. She's dead and gone, victim of suicide. You're simply getting background on everything to write a book on the historic and tragic story. You may be able to get more out of people than a detective or even a private eye could."

"You want me to play an undercover sleuth?" I was still trying to digest his proposal. I also sensed my spirits suddenly reviving from the shock of the past week.

I had thought that Greta may have been murdered, not fully buying that she killed herself. But I had pushed that suspicion to the back of my mind. I only knew what I'd been told and read. She purposely drowned. I had no details.

Antonelli watched me patiently. Finally, he said, "Are we on the same page, Frank?"

I stood. "I think I'll head back down to Baltimore in the morning," I said.

We shook hands. As I was walking to the door, he called me back.

"One more thing, Frank. You'll have a collaborator in your research---in your sleuthing. I'll give you his cell number. Contact him this week."

I looked at him waiting for more to go on.

"His name is Robert Grazer. He's called 'Buffalo Bob,' by those who know him. When I was the Baltimore's GM I hired him to find out who was the locker room thief some ten years ago. Someone had been pilfering personal items from the players lockers. Turned out to be one of the female groupies that hung around the team. Women have come a long way. That one broke the glass ceiling on lock pickers."

"He's a private investigator?"

"A very peculiar one. As a writer, you'll probably like him. If nothing else he'll give you more color for the book. You'll make a good team. And he's got connections. You've got your cover and he'll find his."

"Does Phil Gazzetti know of my revised assignment?"

"No one knows, but you, me, and Buffalo Bob. Gazzetti shouldn't know. He could be a suspect."

"I see," I said, not really seeing it.

"Frank, we don't want players who could be persons of interest to clam up over the circumstances surrounding her death. We also don't want the media to get the drift that MLB suspects foul play. If they pick it up there'll be undue pressure on me to back off, to let the narrative of suicide ride. All those factions that smeared her. They don't want Greta to be a victim of murder who might become a martyr. They want her to be a victim of herself."

I began to realize that Antonelli was dead set on investigating a murder.

"Frank, the team owners all around the league would pressure me to pull back, fearing it would create bad publicity that could hurt everyone, particularly if another player was behind it."

I raised my eyebrows. His comments gave me much to muse on while driving back to Hoboken.

Chapter 25

I met up with Buffalo Bob Grazer in his row house the day after I arrived back at Baltimore's Waterfront Hotel. His living space was odd in its design. The kitchen where we ended up conversing was on the second floor, accessible by a steep, narrow stairway. The living room was also on the second floor in the front of the house. I first got the impression that Buffalo Bob lived alone; but as I went to sit down on one of the chairs at the kitchen table, he wagged his finger at me, and pointed for me to sit in another chair. I followed his silent directions.

"My father sits there," he said.

It was curious to me how Grazer got his nickname. He had a big head, bald on top with a lot of frizzy, gray-streaked hair puffing out on his sides. The head could be imagined as the head of an American bison. To me the animal looked dumb and Buffalo Bob often seemed obtuse. The more I engaged in conversation with this man, the more I found myself baffled by him and whatever he was saying.

"You and your father share this row house?" I asked.

"No, he's dead."

I was baffled at that.

"Oh, I'm sorry. How long ago did he pass?"

"About twenty years ago," he said to me and then to the chair he indicated where his father sits.

Then Buffalo Bob got up, jostled that chair back from the table, and smiled at it before sitting back down. Street noise came in loudly from an opened window in the front living room: a far-off din and the hissing sound of a truck braking close by.

"How long have you been doing private investigation?" I asked.

"On and off," was all he said.

There was no confidence building in me yet for collaborating with this man.

He got up and walked out of the room to another room with a door. He disappeared behind it and was back quickly carrying a briefcase which he put down on the kitchen table beside him.

"You're probably wondering if I have credentials," he said, continuing with a solemn look on his face. "My brother is a homicide detective on the force. He takes after my dad, here," he said, looking at the empty chair. "Dad retired from the DA's office just before he left us."

He had a goofy seriousness about his manner.

"I guess you know of my assignment."

"You will be asking questions around the clubhouse about Greta for your book, looking to find clues to her murder."

"That's what I've been asked to do."

"You're like – " he said and broke out giggling. "You're like Arthur – " he said, and the giggling took over again. "You're – " he tried again, but the giggling kept surfacing like the effervescence in a soda bottle that's been shaken.

Then he started cackling at the humor playing out in his head and I had no clue what it was.

"So, you believe she was murdered," I said trying to ground him.

"Ho, ho, oh I'm sorry. Sometimes I got these funny thoughts that crack me up before I can share them. Sorry, well, um, hey, maybe she was into masochism, the kinky stuff. Either way, there are simpler ways of killing yourself. Women usually overdose or slit their wrists."

"What did you mean by 'masochism?' " I asked.

"Well, now," he began fidgeting with his coffee cup. "You know, if she was found in a position that is ul-tra-submissive. Sure, she could have done it to herself. Yep, I can imagine her naked, stepping into the sauna, getting on her knees, to show her beautiful ass, but no one watching? Then she would have had to fasten the chain that choked her to the tub somehow. With her head trapped at the bottom, she would have had to reach up to the faucet. No, I don't see it. I put my money on a killer who surprised her, covered her face with ether. He would have lifted her into the tub, wrapped the chain round her neck, held her tight to the drain and ran the water.

"Or! She was into kink with someone she trusted, some psychopath who led her effortlessly into the tub and tied her down. What do you say? You knew her, no? Do you think she was into kink with someone?"

I felt baffled, or buffaloed, once more. What was he talking about? It seemed like wild conjecture.

"Are you just – "

He cut in, "Oh, she had a body. I've seen her legs. Whoa!" He was smiling lasciviously, then his smile turned grim. "I bet she was a good girl.

"The killer must have surprised her."

"Bob, what you are talking about? The reports in the media suggested she willfully drowned in the tub. Is this just a theory of yours?" I was eager to hear information that validated my instinct Greta would not commit suicide.

His look suggested he was growing impatient with me. He got up, went to the kitchen counter and in a moment, I heard a sizzling and then the popping of popcorn.

"The force of gravity is a theory. I deal in more than intuition, I assure you."

With this statement, he opened his briefcase. In it was a baseball mitt. He lifted the mitt and pulled out a folder, laying it before me.

I turned open the folder. Inside were sheets from a copier machine showing color images of a lifeless Greta, one showed her body lain on a massage table. Her skin had the pallor of death, her lips purplish, her eyes staring up, frozen. A red mark cut clear across her neck contrasting with the pale skin. A red mark that broke the skin here and there.

The other photo showed her backside, and her face by the drain of the sauna.

"Where did you get these?"

"Oh, I have sources. Don't doubt that."

I studied the pictures as dispassionately as possible. We already buried her. The gruesome images of her dead body did not allow me any connection to the young woman I'd known when full of life. I didn't want there to be a connection.

A bowl of popcorn was slid onto the table. Buffalo Bob indulged, throwing the fluffy kernels one by one into his mouth. As good as the popcorn smelled, I passed.

As I was walking out the front door and down the front steps, Buffalo Bob was right behind me, wheeling a retro bicycle, the kind with the thick wheels, his baseball mitt hooked onto the handlebar. As he rode away, he called back, "I've got a game!"

As peculiar as I found Bob to be, he had produced big time in our first meeting. The images I saw had not been printed or alluded to in the *Sun* or the *Reporter*. The public did not know they existed.

Chapter 26

I prowled the team's clubhouse early Wednesday afternoon, about the same time of day Greta would have arrived there to sauna and get a massage. A couple people came in and out: the laundry attendant, placing uniforms and undergarments in each player's open locker; and later two massage specialists, followed by the players who wanted their muscles and ligaments worked on.

When assistant trainer Earl McCoy walked in he was soon working on a player's thighs and knees on the massage table, leaving me no opening to approach. Likewise with the massage specialists. Other players took early sauna baths. By 4:30 two attendants were laying out catering trays and bringing out food so players could enjoy a hot meal well before game time.

In the video room, pitchers could sit and watch a presentation of the Detroit Tiger batters swinging at pitches. The pitching coach, Lefty Gomez, would hang in and out, eager to discuss a batter's habits.

Relief ace Arny Shelf walked into the video room

and watched fifteen minutes of the batters with Gomez. As the team's "closer," he was likely to see action on any given day. The starting pitcher for tonight's game, Louis Alberto, also joined them. I wanted to speak with Arny, since he may have slept with Greta, given her remarks about him out in San Diego. Frankly, I was a little jealous of him, his youth, his strapping physique, his good looks. She was dead and I still had this insecure feeling that I guess any older man would have.

When Arny left the video room he entered into the hospitality hall to grab something to eat. I stepped in beside him with a plate in hand.

"They treat you guys like kings here," I said, trying to break into a casual conversation with him.

"I've asked them if they could deliver finger food to the mound in between batters," he quipped.

I smiled at the remark. "How is everybody the past couple weeks?" I asked, alluding to Greta's death.

"Some of us were affected more than others."

Just then Monk Morton tooled in with his usual, confidant waddle.

"Wally worked with her more than anyone. Think he was a little sweet on her too," Arny said.

"And you?"

He took the question only one way. "I got to know her a little bit in the pen. Girl was into pitching."

I wondered if it mattered much who had slept with Greta. It could matter, especially if one of them felt spurned. Of course, a player who had not gotten her in bed could also have felt rejected by her. I wanted to think all the players fell into that category, everyone striking out with her. But since seeing the pictures of her corpse and listening to Buffalo Bob's imaginative speculations on the circumstances of her death, my own mind went wild at the possibilities of Greta's activities with teammates, ranging from promiscuity to nymphomania to sadomasochism.

In death, Greta remained a puzzle to me. I really had nothing certain to go on about other relationships she may have had. It was clear she was all pitcher and all girl at the same time. Just as clearly the other players were all baseball, all boy. Athletics juiced sexual readiness, didn't dull the drive. I did my best to rationalize Greta away from them. I took comfort in thinking that if Greta had been sleeping around she would not have landed in my room. It's true I was too old for her no matter how you counted the years between us, no matter how attractive this face she likened to a Civil War general, no matter how it might have been framed by a girl who missed her daddy. Still, despite the years between us and all the virile men around her, she had come to my bed.

I was guilty of being unfair to Greta's memory. In her

death, I was wildly jealous thinking how far ranging her relationships may have been.

When I saw an opportunity to engage with Zorro Negrewski at his locker I asked him, "What was it like on first base when Greta was pitching," as I imagined how he watched her sweet thigh swinging around to him.

"Still on that book, man?" Negrewski said in his husky, Russian accent.

"I am. The commissioner wants me to follow through, get a player's thoughts in the aftermath."

"Well, she was a sly one. She kept runners close. She kept batters off stride."

Did you sleep with her, Zorro, is what I wanted to ask, but I felt at a loss at what I could or should say.

"Did you know her off the field, much?" I asked discreetly.

"Some of us took her out for a drink, once. She was shy. Believe it? She dressed to kill, but she was sweet and shy. Whoever killed her couldn't have known her."

So here was one player going against the media narrative. I was excited to follow up on his comment. "What do you mean, couldn't have known her."

"Had to be some uptight psycho who never met her, or couldn't get close. Hey, I'm an amateur shrink. Don't listen to me." With that he turned his back to me to undress and change into his uniform.

I saw Gilbert Rue at his locker and walked up to it.

"Hello, Frank, still working on that book? I thought you'd have wrapped it up."

"Getting more comments from players. There may be a different perspective since Greta's death."

"It's a shame. She needed God in her life. She was full of the devil ... and the devil killed her." He spoke with a chilling certainty.

"Why do you think she did not have God in her life?"

"If you have Jesus in your life, you don't dress to sleep with every Tom, Dick, and Harry." Rue stretched his arms into his jersey. "I'll pray for her soul tonight."

Was Rue the kind of uptight guy Negrewski was referring to, I wondered.

I thought to approach Manager Ralston in his office. I went into the hallway, passing a door with a sign that read: Auxiliary Lockers. This was where the ball girls dressed. Greta had also dressed with them the first week she was called up, before the team gave her a private room and sauna. I knocked on the door. A young lady in t-shirt and jeans opened it and I introduced myself.

"Yeah, I know who you are. You're the writer." And that gave me the opening to be invited in to ask a few questions. Another ball girl was just tying up her cleats. She had the boyish haircut. The one inviting me in had long hair pulled into a pony tail. Both girls were tall, five nine or so. The one with the pony tail was lanky, the other stocky.

"Did you share this room with Greta Reich when she was called up?"

"Sure did. The first week. Then she got the star treatment. Gave her her own locker room and sauna. Maybe she'd still be alive today if they hadn't."

"How do you mean?"

"Nothing, really. Maybe she wouldn't have had the kind of privacy that led to her drowning."

"Do you think she drowned herself?" I asked.

The ball girl with boyish haircut interjected, "Looks that way to some. It's a violent way to go. She must have had a lot of self-loathing. Look at the way she dressed. Is that self-respect?"

I itched to get out of that room, wanting fresh air badly. I couldn't bear hearing remarks about self-loathing when I knew that Greta loved life and herself enough to want to enjoy it as much as possible.

"I pitch too," the girl with the pony tail said.

"Yeah?" I said.

"I'm faster than Greta was. I'm thinking I should ask for a tryout."

If she was faster than Greta she would probably get clobbered by minor league or major league bats. She would have to have incredible English on the ball and a baffling array of pitches for any chance to survive in the minors.

"Why not," I said. "What have you got to lose?"

Ralston was in his managerial cave down the hallway. Looking through the window to his office I saw he was in conversation with another man who sported a handlebar mustache. Ralston waived me in.

"Frank, you know Ed Farley."

I knew of the Club's owner. Notorious playboy, flamboyant sportsman. Besides a major league team, he owned race horses, the city's arena, and dated high-society women, all young.

"Pleased to meet you, Mr. Farley. Frank Barr."

"Yes, the commissioner spoke to me about you. Are you done with your research on the book?"

"Not yet. The commissioner thought it would be a good idea to get players' perspectives on Greta in the aftermath of her time here."

"Well, good luck with it. Ralston wants to keep the team focused on the here and now. Little Greta was great; but she was a freak of nature, a big distraction. May she rest in peace."

Farley's dismissal of Greta as someone who was just a distraction surprised me.

"I wouldn't mind having that little spitfire on the mound tonight to face these Tiger bats, I'll tell you," said

Ralston. "But she's gone. Ed's right. We need to focus on the here and now."

"I won't interfere with that. I'm almost done getting background from players. I believe the commissioner is hoping for a book that covers more than just the games, her pitching, and the like; but more of what she meant to baseball, to the country. It's a tall order," I said, smiling. "Thanks for putting up with me."

"You're a fine writer, Barr," Farley said. "You're right in your books that todays' game needs more soul, as you put it. But baseball's a business. Always has been. Money drives the game. Always has. Just that times are different from the glory years you pine about."

Farley was looking up at me, his tongue wagging in his open mouth in a condescending manner. "But good luck on this new book. Hope you a sell a million," he added, perhaps insinuating we were both members of the money-making club. In that, he would not have been wrong.

When I walked out onto the field two groundskeepers were rolling out the batting cage so that the players could take their practice swings against pitched balls. Next thing I knew the ball girl with the pony tail was running up to me. "Frank, could you watch me throw some pitches, see what you think?"

She recruited the second-string catcher to warm her

up for my sake along the first base line in foul territory. She associated me with Greta's rise and figured if I was impressed it could help her cause for a tryout. I ambled closer to where the catcher squatted behind a plate in the ground. The ball girl toed a rubber in the dirt and began winding up and tossing the ball. Like Greta, she too was a lefty. With eight pitches, she gave the catcher a good work out. Her pitches came in at a moderate speed, faster than Greta perhaps, but still slow by major league standards. The problem was she had poor control. The catcher was leaping all over to pull in the ball. Another pitcher had sidled up beside her, signaling he wanted warm-up time with the catcher. She walked over to me.

"Well, what do you think?"

"You got promise." I didn't have the heart to tell her anything else.

Chapter 27

I watched the game using my special pass to sit in a box seat along the first base line. I watched the ball being pitched, the batters swinging and running, and the fielders catching most of the balls on the fly. But I didn't care how they played or who won. I took in the atmosphere of the summer night around me, listened to drunken fans heckling the Tigers; but took no comfort in the geometry of the field or the order of the game, the things that normally would give me a sense of security about the chaotic world.

I sat watching five innings of a low-scoring game itching to leave the park. I was alone watching a ballgame and I could only think about the moments I had enjoyed a game with my wife. She thoroughly enjoyed herself rooting for the home team, each pitch, each play, each player, and I loved just watching her be excited. So, I thought back to her. Thoughts of Greta would only touch on the despair suppressed inside me. The night's game accented the fact I was alone, and I don't know who won it.

I cabbed it to a cigar club located two blocks from the Waterfront, hoping to enjoy a fine cigar on the bar's patio in the summer air. My wife had enjoyed me having this pleasure up until the final year when she didn't enjoy much of anything about me anymore.

I savored the tobacco in my palate and the smoke I would gently blow into the air while sipping a high-end cognac. The cognac seeped into my brain and I thought of the pleasures I'd had with a nineteen-year old sexpot whose existence I'd found astonishing. Her improbable success as a pitcher in the big leagues was now as unbelievable as her physical beauty. I would think of Greta and the moments we shared and yet my mind would drift back to my wife, the woman with whom I enjoyed over twenty years of companionship. The sex with Greta had been phenomenal but I realized thinking back on it that I didn't know her. I couldn't reflect on much about her other than she knew how to hold a baseball several ways, loved to cuss and speak her mind, and loved to drive herself to an orgasm. She missed her daddy and that was what drove her to me. There was no more connection than that. Never having raised a daughter, I could not even relate to her as a surrogate father.

I puffed away and asked myself what I was doing in Baltimore now. I was no sleuth. I did not even like interviewing people. I never did. All the years I covered sports for the *Reporter*, it was the one part of the job I didn't relish, engaging with all the personalities, the spoiled players, the shallow players, the boring players. This afternoon I had talked to several of them, gingerly walking around the subject of Greta's death. The case needed hard detective work, background checks on persons of interest, cat-and-mouse tactics with anyone suspected of such a horrible crime. I was out of my league.

In the morning, I phoned Phil Gazzetti and asked if I could meet with him. He obliged and I found myself having a cup of coffee with him mid-morning.

"I hear you're still getting background on Greta Reich with the players."

"The commissioner wants to capture the big picture of what happened here when she played. Not just the balls and strikes, but what it all meant."

"How much more time you need here, you think?"

"A few more days perhaps. I'll stay though this homestand."

"Funny how things turned," he said.

"Started out as an amazing story, history in the making," I said.

"Then overnight she became a social pariah."

"She was prey to all the ugly forces in this country."

"And she couldn't take it."

"You don't believe she took her own life, do you?" I asked him, remembering the commissioner's words and knowing I shouldn't tread on this subject.

"Hate to say it, but she was out of her league. She was an exhibitionist who loved drawing attention but was ambushed by all the hate. I should have cut her loose the first sign of trouble."

I was seething inside. It was Gazzetti who had put her out for all the attention. It was Gazzetti who had set her up for the *Untouchable* cover that smeared her reputation.

He continued, "But your book will be good for baseball and good for the ball club, no?" Gazzetti's ego escorted his next words. "With the perspective of time, Greta Reich will shine as the game's most amazing episode."

"And you'll be associated with her." Why I continued to stroke him is beyond me.

I walked out the building and onto the brick concourse of Eutaw Street behind the right field bleachers, gazing onto the green outfield. I didn't sense the excitement of the game to be played that night. I just felt the emptiness of the field. Then I felt someone poking me gently in both kidneys. Kate Bower stepped alongside me.

"I saw you last night watching the game."

"Yes."

"Tell me next time. I'll join you."

"My heart wasn't in it. I left early."

"I know."

"Sorry."

"You miss her?" She asked. I assumed she meant Greta, maybe even suspected my involvement with her beyond the interviews.

"I miss everything that was alive in my life."

"Hey, let's walk." She grabbed my arm and led me out of ball park and onto the street. Then we were walking onto a beautiful hardwood floor past framed posters reflecting America's zany history of pop culture. We explored the various objects inside Geppi's Museum, from toy robots to models of Superman.

"I put on hospitality events here, once for the player's families. Another a reception for the writers and broadcasters." Kate was smiling broadly, doing her best to take me away from the funk she found me in. She grabbed my arm again and took me a couple blocks to a pub where we sat for lunch. Kate ordered meatloaf, fries, and a beer. Not wanting to think too much about it, I ordered what she did.

She was in the middle of describing this novel she was reading when she turned on a dime and asked, "Do you ever think of adopting children?"

I smiled, amused, eyeing her quizzically. "You're not

proposing, are you Kate?"

She laughed heartily.

"Just wondering. I missed my chance, so I think about it. Could you see yourself as a father?"

"Well, I thought for a long time I wanted to be a father. Like my father, you know. But now? I don't know. It's a young man's game, isn't it? Besides, adults get very selfish just tending to their own needs all their lives. Don't you think?"

"I suppose," she sighed.

"Could you see yourself chasing a toddler around the living room floor, or spending time with an eight-year-old over homework?"

"Do you like D.H. Lawrence, his poetry?" she said, changing the subject.

After the meal, we walked back to the Camden Yards warehouse. She took the elevator up to the executive offices. I walked out and over to the ballpark and down into the clubhouse. There in the room housing massage tables, saunas, and exercise contraptions with pulleys and weights, I found the team's head trainer, Rene Corcoran. He wore a trainer's uniform, a purple polo shirt with the Baltimore Club insignia on its chest, and white pants with the Club's purple stripe down the sides. He was six-foot tall and lean, looking all sinew, muscle, tendon and ligament, no fat. His face was angular and bony. His relaxed state of conversation was as taut as his body.

After a minute of small talk, I threw him the question I'd been waiting to ask him: "Rene, did Greta Reich get her arm worked on here the day she died?"

He frowned, seemed to think on the question a moment and said, "I don't believe so. When I got here she was already dead."

"Who found her?"

"Well, that my friend, is a question you'd have to ask the police."

I thought of pushing it further but he glided out of the room, moving like a thin blade that sliced through the air.

Chapter 28

"I'm thinking Ed Farley killed her."

I was sitting at Buffalo Bob Grazer's kitchen table. He was leaning against the sink, drinking coffee out of a ceramic cup. My cup was in hand. I looked up at him waiting for him to say something more preposterous. At the same time, I wondered if his crazy intuitions drew on any sharp logic that would escape most minds.

"Farley's a rascal. Dates young girls."

I interjected a comment of reason into his reality. "Takes more than a rascal to murder."

"Like being on a joy ride to some."

I played along. "Motive?"

"He owned her. Had her under contract. But she was an independent little tomboy. Probably spurned his advances. He took revenge."

If figuring out who the killer was as simple as this, there were plenty of suspects that could have the psychological motive, but for murder?

"You called me here to tell me you think it was the

team's owner?"

Just then the doorbell rang, actually a buzzer. Bob went down the stairs. He came back up with a man following him. The man wore a brown jacket and tie loosened around the neck and black pants. His head was balding, his mustache salt and pepper.

"Tommy, this is Frank Barr."

The man stuck out his hand as I stood. "Tom Grazer. I read *Game of Catch*. You hit the nail on the head. Game ain't what it used to be."

"Tommy's the detective on the force I told you about."

He sat and Bob handed him a cup of coffee.

"My kid brother has kept me in the loop on your assignment for the commissioner."

I wasn't sure what Tom Grazer was here for but I had one big question for him.

"Detective, why isn't there an ongoing investigation into the murder of Greta Reich?"

Tom looked over to his brother leaning against the sink drinking his coffee and back to me.

"Off the record, Frank. The case isn't closed, but our hands have been tied ever since the mayor met with the chief after she was buried. The word is she told the chief to focus in on other pressing crimes at hand, ones that were indisputable murders."

"Do you believe Greta Reich was murdered?"

"It looks more like a murder than a suicide, if that's what you're asking."

"Why would the mayor tell the police to lay off investigating such a high-profile case?"

Tom Grazer looked at me with exasperated eyes. "If you can figure out all the politics going on in this country today, clue me in. I don't know. I do know the mayor is way out in left field and is known as a progressive feminist. The feminists hated Greta Reich."

"Did anyone question the obvious persons of interest who would have been in the clubhouse at the time of her death?"

"Yes, one officer and myself, conducted routine questioning. But the usual follow-up was blocked. Off the record Frank, my kid brother is doing some legwork, keeping me in the loop."

I wondered how much faith Tom had in his brother to effectively snoop. Tom detected this question in my look.

"Bob may say some absurd things, you might think, but he's more wily than he lets on."

He handed me his card. "Keep Bob in the know on anything you find out or suspect. Don't hesitate to call me as well. Once there's a scent, I'll get involved. Officially."

He rose to leave, kissing his brother on his forehead.

I rose and had to say it. "Your brother thinks Ed Farley killed her."

The detective smiled, looked over to Bob, and then responded. "Yeah, I can see it." Then he was gone down the steps and out the front door.

I thought to call Buffalo Bob the next morning, telling him I wanted to go over a few things on the case. He asked me to meet him at a quaint café in Fells Point, Baltimore's waterfront neighborhood that was unblemished by national chain stores or restaurants, and full of independent pubs and shops. Its docks were used by tugboats.

Bob just went for black coffee and so did I. The common preference didn't escape him.

"You and I both like black coffee," he said. "We got to find that out about the killer."

"Whether he likes black coffee or latte?"

"Something like that, but I was thinking more like, what other kind of submission methods he might prefer, maybe dog collars."

"Hmm. Well, I wanted to discuss more basic inquiries. Like checking the other attendants in the clubhouse, what they might have seen. For instance, when did they see the trainer come in. The head trainer told me he didn't get to the clubhouse until after Greta was found dead."

Buffalo Bob took to rubbing his chin with his thumb for a minute, mulling over what I'd shared. "I'll look into this," was all he said.

"Also, we need to find out if the scout, Pete Sake, was in town at the time of her murder. This is important. I have reason to believe he had motive."

"Pete Sake, huh?" He was rubbing his chin again. "What would be the motive?"

"I can't divulge it now. Something that Greta confided in me. I need–we need–to know if Sake was in town the day before and on the day of the murder."

"You got it."

When we got up to leave, Bob lifted his bike from against the wall and began pedaling once outside the door. The sight of this overgrown kid on his retro bike with thick tires weaving among pedestrians, past all the shops and then by the red tugboats at the docks, had me thinking of Norman Rockwell illustrations. As interesting as this was to me as a writer, I just didn't know how effective a Norman Rockwell character could be as a private eye on a real murder case.

Chapter 29

I was determined to confront the police commissioner. The more I thought about Tom Grazer's tip that the case was virtually dropped after the Chief met with the Mayor, I was beside myself. That one meeting was at the heart of what was wrong with the entire world. People wielded power with their emotions wrapped around self-interest, ignoring any sense of what was right or wrong. In the world of politics, they acted in concert with the wishes of the people they were beholden to. The mayor felt beholden to the progressive liberals who were the base of her support. The chief was beholden to the mayor who appointed him, and on a whim could put someone else in his place.

Before I sought out the commissioner I wanted ammunition beyond the photocopied images of her corpse. I sought out the head of psychology at John Hopkins University. I drove west, way out of town past the zoo, until I reached the campus. The Psych Department was temporarily shifted to an old row house across from the main campus, while the current one was being renovated.

I walked up the stoop of the row house and couldn't help being reminded of Buffalo Bob's home.

The head of the Psych Department held her office in a small, upstairs bedroom, or what had once been a bedroom. There was a steam-heat radiator against one wall. She wore black, broad-rim glasses, had long brown hair, was attractive and in her late forties. She looked up at me with a stifled smile. I knocked on the wooden door frame and was invited in.

It turned out she had season tickets to Camden Yards and we talked a little baseball as we got through the small talk of introductions. It didn't hurt that she read *Game of Catch*. After complimenting me on the book she began ruminating on our sports-drenched, fan-based society.

"Mr. Barr, I couldn't agree with you more how professional sports has turned the public into a society of spectators. How it's damaged the people's ability to function." She stuck with the formal address of Mr. Barr, and I addressed her as Dr. Ravin.

"And I loved, Mr. Barr, your reference to Muammar Gaddafi, of all people. How he banned spectator activities from Libya and because of it, society there was more participatory. Healthier. Unfortunately, his end was not a just reward."

"Well, Dr. Ravin, you might say his people participated in his demise."

"I'm afraid so. So, tell me, how may I help you?"

I told her how I was commissioned to write a book on Greta Reich and baseball's historic moment. I covered briefly how Greta was castigated by the media for speaking her mind, and then spoke about her death. I wanted her professional opinion of the likelihood of Greta committing suicide. I laid on her desk the photocopies, the one where she's submissively positioned in the tub, the other where she is lain on the massage table, red marks visible across her neck.

"What are the chances she took this violent path to killing herself?"

Dr. Ravin looked down on the two photocopies on her desk before her. "The reports in the papers called it a suicide," she remarked, studying the images.

She finally looked up at me, silent.

"Does a young woman use a violent means to kill herself?" I asked.

"Well," she said, eyeing me, seemingly irked by something. "No one person is alike, Mr. Barr. Greta Reich may have been filled with self-loathing. She was an exhibitionist who craved attention. But society didn't give her the adulation she wanted. It spurned her. No wonder. She was an apologist for rape, for God's sake. And that magazine cover! The Confederate flag! My God!"

It was obvious to me that Dr. Ravin had a political perspective on Greta's episodes with the team, and her death.

"Isn't it true that women take their own life by overdosing on pills or sometimes by slitting their wrists? The act of drowning oneself forcibly does not seem to fit that profile."

"You don't need me for statistics, Mr. Barr. I've given you my opinion. I think it's very possible she hated herself and planned a violent end."

I looked at the credenza behind her at the two framed photos. One was a black and white picture of an older couple with gray hair. Perhaps her parents. The other photo was that of a woman with blond hair, perhaps her age. There were no photos of children or a possible husband. I concluded I would not get an opinion I could attribute to her that would be helpful.

I hoped for a better meeting downtown. The police commissioner held office a block from City Hall on East Fayette Street. I figured the photocopied images in my possession would be enough of a jolt to persuade him to change tact on investigating Greta's murder.

Ray Strauss was a white commissioner in charge of a police force more black than white. The last commissioner, black, was facing a trial and corruption charges. Strauss was the mayor's only white appointee. He had been a captain on the force for twenty years. The promotion tripled his pay and brought him more prestige. It gave him more of an "executive" future should he ever leave the force.

I had walked into headquarters and up to an officer sipping a cup of coffee, standing, chatting with another officer at his desk. "I'm looking for Chief Strauss," I said.

"That would be me," he answered directly. "How may I help you."

"Frank Barr. The commissioner of baseball assigned me to write on book on the Greta Reich story. I have a couple questions I'd like to ask you."

"Come into my office," he said behind an exaggerated grin.

When I was seated in a hard wooden chair on the other side of his desk, I saw his prominent belly bulge below his chest. His face had the red glow of a drinker. I got right to the point.

"Chief Strauss, Greta Reich's story–the end of it right now is clouded in mystery. My sources tell me that you've side-railed the investigation into her murder."

Strauss didn't blink. He took his time considering a response.

"I don't know what you've heard. I will say that there are several investigations ongoing into murders. Some very brutal murders. Greta Reich's cause of death was inconclusive. We know she drowned. Suicide was not ruled out. There were no signs of struggle."

I chose that moment to lay the photocopies before him. He looked at them silently for a good minute.

"I see your source has roots inside this building."

I said nothing and the Chief continued. "Still, suicide was not ruled out."

"Chief, I'll be forthright. The word on the street is that the mayor asked you to have the force stand down on the Reich investigation, indefinitely."

"I'm sure you don't write based on rumors alone," he came back at me. "I remember when you wrote a sports column for the *Reporter*. Then you had latitude and license to lean in with your opinions. Very entertaining, I recall. I have a busy day planned. Is there anything else I can help you with?"

I felt the anger rise up in me. I was now fighting for right against wrong as much as for Greta's legacy. "Chief, Greta Reich and baseball deserve a complete investigation. I still have contacts at the *Sun*. I'm hoping you'll sidestep any political pressure and do the right thing here."

The chief looked away, swung his chair round to face the window that looked onto the War Memorial Plaza, a public square in front of City Hall and police headquarters.

Chief Strauss swung back to face me. "I will assess where we are in all the investigations. I will go over the Reich case with the investigating officers. Should I decide to press forward, I'm sure your source will let you know."

"Thank you for your time, Chief," I said curtly, rising to go.

"Well, thank you for advocating on behalf of Miss Reich," he said with an alligator smile.

I left without any confidence the Chief would reopen the investigation. He struck me as an example of the Peter Principle, one who rises to his level of incompetence, only to be kicked farther up the ladder. In elevating such a professional, the mayor could assure that he'd be dependent on her. Maybe I was wrong and he'd surprise me.

In my hotel that night I ordered room service for dinner and watched the news on the TV. Later I watched a half-hour program devoted to Greta, her surprise rise to MLB, her stunning success, and then the pariah she became. A couple weeks after she was buried the media was still defaming her.

I missed her. I didn't miss her in the way I sometimes longed for the comfortable companionship of my ex-wife. I missed the explosion of feeling alive with Greta. We spent nights and mornings wrapped together. I missed the ecstasy of consuming her body and breath.

Greta gave me an invigorating sense of youth I hadn't felt in decades. I was still feeling the withdrawal symptoms.

I thought of the old man in the movie, *Damn Yankees*, who makes a deal with the devil to be a baseball player and young again. Then in the last scene, he is running down a fly ball in centerfield, just as the time the devil granted him has run out, and he is quickly aging during the play and stumbling to the ground, an old man once again. The days after Greta died I felt I was aging faster than ever. I felt it in my walk. I saw it in the mirror.

Chapter 30

Life becomes more interesting when a woman begins pursuing you. Especially when the woman is good-humored, sometimes girlish, and good-looking. When the Baseball Club went back on the road, Kate Bower called and invited me to a Saturday night theater performance. I put off going back up to Hoboken for the date.

Kate wasn't shy about showing her interest in me. She tickled, teased, and edged into intimate talk about the little preferences one has in life. She was fun to be around and this may be why I was finding her more physically attractive each time around with her. I noticed she was slimming down a bit which highlighted the curves in her hips and torso. She was a full-figured woman at five foot, four inches tall, with a lot of hip and a lot of breast. She was a little wide around the waist and that had diminished some. But it was her smile that overwhelmed her appearance.

It was flattering being eyed by an attractive woman. I looked forward to being with her for the play, which to my surprise was about a funeral. Had I known this beforehand I may have begged off, as Greta's burial was too fresh in my mind.

The theater was in an old, renovated bank building close to City Hall. I think it had been developed sometime after I had left Baltimore. Along one wall was a bar promoted as the "Longest Bar in Baltimore." Everyone milled about the bar the hour before the play began, during intermission, and after the performance. The audience sat in solid wooden chairs, the kind used long ago in schools. There was a stage and on it was a pinewood casket.

The setting of the play was an Irish wake. A body lay in the casket, presumably dead, that came to life midway through the performance. Members of the audience were recruited to participate. The whole evening became a raucous affair suited for a beer hall, the beer being a major participant. People normally try to relax at a wake, smile, and laugh a little. This wake had people standing and shouting. Even the dead man in the coffin was stirred to rise and let his feelings known.

Kate wrapped her arm around mine during most of the performance. I definitely felt taken. At my age, it was also a feeling of being saved.

It was during intermission when I noticed the ball girl, the one with the short, boyish haircut. She wore a tan blazer and black trousers and stood with another young woman in her twenties dressed in a sleeveless blouse and long skirt. Her light brown hair was short but cut in a girlish style. She wore a silver-gray chain necklace.

Kate and I walked to the bar during the intermission. Both of us had a second beer there and munched on peanuts. I motioned farther down the bar. "You recognize the ball girl?"

"No? Which one?"

"The dyke-ish one."

"That's not nice," she scolded me gently. "You mean Grendel?"

"Yes."

Kate raised her head up to look down the bar. She got up and walked quickly to the two girls and spoke with them briefly and came back.

"I just wanted to say hi. She's with her girlfriend, I think."

"I think so."

"Well, to each his own," Kate said, raising her beer mug to click mine.

After the play was over we got in Kate's little, compact car and drove to a Canton neighborhood café for coffee and biscotti. Its quiet atmosphere was a welcome contrast to the boisterous theater we left. It gave us a chance to talk with each other for the first time that evening.

"Ever attend an Irish wake, Kate? You're of Irish descent, no?"

"Yes, and yes. I'm also a bit Dutch," she said, her eyes twinkling, as if the Dutch blood gave her character more panache. "My mother. My father's mother was Italian. The whole blend makes me somewhat saucy."

"Sexy," I added.

"Tell me more," she said, smiling.

"I've said all I can at this point in time."

She was looking hard into my eyes. "Your eyes are dreamy," she said.

"I've been told."

We played with one another with words, enjoying the coffee and biscotti. Then Kate drove me back to the Waterfront Hotel. "Thanks for a great evening, Kate. I'll sleep good tonight," I said, signaling that I was ready to turn in. She looked at me, hesitating, then leaned over and kissed me gently on the mouth.

Only a few days later, while I was back in my flat in Hoboken, I got another call from Kate. She wanted me to come to her place for dinner. "I'm a pretty good cook," she said. I told her I'd drive back down Saturday morning.

Friday morning, when I turned on my tablet to scan the nation's newspapers, there was a big headline on the front page of the *Reporter*: CENTER FIELDER JAILED IN ATLANTA. Indeed, news was splashed all over the nation's papers that the Club's centerfielder, Gilbert Rue, was arrested for sexual assault on a woman in a bar in downtown Atlanta, where the team was playing the Braves. Paper to paper the details were sketchy, a sorry trait of twenty-first century journalism. One account reported that Rue had menacingly placed his hand on the woman's throat. Another said he had twisted her arm behind her back. It was all hearsay. What seemed certain was that Rue was arrested. It wasn't clear if he spent the night in jail or only minutes before team management bailed him out.

To my disgust, several of the papers implied that Greta Reich's anti-rape comments were allegedly responsible for Rue acting out. I phoned Kate to get more on it. She knew even less than I did. The story was too fresh.

The saddest part about the story was that Rue was married with children. Guilty or not, his name and reputation was under siege. I was ambivalent about whether it was true or not. There were women today lying in wait to ambush professional athletes with such charges. They might make such a story up entirely or stretch the truth to suit their goals, which were often mercenary. Some of these women were mental basket cases. It was hard to sift through these stories to determine which merited belief because the facts, sources, and writing were so murky most of the time. I always sensed Rue, the mild-mannered, born-again Christian, was wound too tight. Behind his passive demeanor might stalk a monster.

"We'll see how it plays out," I said to myself while I shifted to the game news in the sports section. The Baseball Club lost to the Braves that night and still struggled in the standings. Arny Shelf came into the last inning only to give up a grand slam homer to lose it.

I called Buffalo Bob and asked him if he knew from his brother if the chief had unleashed the investigation into Greta's murder. He hadn't heard that he did.

I drove back down to Baltimore late Friday. I wanted to feel fresh when I went to Kate's place the next day.

Saturday morning from my room in the Waterfront Hotel, I scoured the online papers again.

Rue had spent a couple hours in a holding cell before being bailed out. He claimed the charge was bogus and that he barely spoke to the woman at the bar. Of course, being a married man, you expected him to say something of this sort.

I looked into my wallet to see if I had kept Rolly Singer's business card from the day we met a few weeks ago. It was there. I hesitated calling him for the purpose I had in mind. I put on my walking sneakers and shorts and took a long walk instead.

I walked ten or more blocks to Fells Point and down the pier the tugboats were tied to. I looked across the water where a few small sailboats were tacking and out across to the old Domino Sugar refinery, an ugly relic of America's manufacturing past built one hundred years ago. The sun was out, but heavy clouds were starting to sail in over the harbor.

I looked across to the modern townhouses some ninety-feet across from this pier. I thought if I ever moved back to Baltimore I would like to live in one, right in the city's most eclectic neighborhood, hobnob around the cafes, pubs, and bookstores, and get to know people. I could afford it now with the money still being generated by the books' sales. I would soon be negotiating with my publisher for a big advance on my Greta book.

I would look at those townhouses, as well as the old row houses in various neighborhoods and wonder what the status of living in desired places was worth to my life. It never added up to happiness if it all meant I'd be living alone. Having new friends in the neighborhood didn't measure up, in my outlook, to counterbalance living alone. You drank a beer with a friend, had coffee with a friend, batted the breeze with a friend, maybe go to a ballgame ... but at the end of the day came home to no one.

Chapter 31

At six I cabbed it to Kate's row house in my old neighborhood, Canton. I didn't want to have to search for a parking space and find one blocks away.

When she opened the door, she was all smiles wearing a red apron and I handed her the bottle of wine I had bought on the way over. She shot a cursory glance at the briefcase I held down by my knees.

Her place was clean but not pristine. Unlike some women I'd met over the years, she had not fashioned the living room into a showroom but an actual room where day-to-day living took place. There were books disheveled on the coffee table by the couch. An umbrella was standing in a corner. She had a few bookcases in the room, so I began browsing while she went back into the kitchen. There was the scent of food cooking that made its way down the hall to me. I smelled tomato sauce. I felt happy she had invited me to dinner.

There were several volumes of poetry on the shelves, and I picked out a volume of Alfred Lord Tennyson. His rhyming verse was old school, but classic, eloquent, clear.

Kate popped in and saw me reading Tennyson. She reached for a notebook on the mantle above the fireplace, opened it to a certain page, and handed it to me. "I wrote this yesterday," she said, and then left the room.

There were six lines scripted by hand in blue ink:

Deep pools in his eyes

Olive-hued

A slight smile on the lips

Sitting on laughter

Rough, warrior's lines

Hide his heart

I looked up. Kate had sat beside me, handing me a glass of the red wine from the bottle I gave her. "I like your poem," I said, sipping the wine.

"It's about you," she said, smiling.

"Am I hiding my heart?"

She sipped her wine, looking over the rim of the glass at me, contemplating the subject at hand.

"What's in the briefcase? Are you going to share poetry you've written?" she asked with a curious eye and a lilt in her voice.

"Not exactly," I said. "After dinner, maybe."

At the mention of dinner, she jumped up and scooted back toward her kitchen. Five minutes later she was back inviting me to sit at the dining table in the kitchen. She had lit two tall candles. A small plate with a salad of assorted vegetables was at both place settings. We sat and Kate smiled, pressed her hands together and said a grace. "Dear Lord, bless this meal and my guest. Thank you for this life."

She smiled at me and I smiled back at her.

The salad consisted of slices of freshly boiled beets, orange slices, leafy greens, a little virgin olive oil, and spices I was trying to discern. It was light and refreshing. The orange citrus flavor complimented the beets amazingly. Kate giggled like a schoolgirl when I told her how great the salad tasted.

The main course was pizza. A pie she made from scratch: dough, sauce, freshly sautéed clams, chosen spices. She had made the sauce from a can of whole tomatoes. She made a dough with two flours, wheat and rice, rice to cut in half the gluten content the wheat added. A heavy dose of gluten in a meal with a lot of pasta or bread could put me to sleep. Maybe Kate wanted to keep me from getting sleepy too early in the evening. I also wondered in the back of my mind if she was going to invite me into her bed later, and if that's where I wanted to be.

Her clam pizza was bursting with rich flavors. I marveled how she was able to make a thin crust. I ate two slices to her one. "Normally, I'd eat three slices, but I'm watching my portions these days," she said.

"Did you like teaching English to college students?" I asked Kate, wanting to learn more about what made her tick.

"I loved teaching literature courses."

"So why did you leave it?"

"I enjoyed the curiosity of the students, but maybe I got tired of the sameness in what I covered year after year. I don't know."

"No scandals that drove you out?" I asked teasingly.

"You know?" she asked with an expression of wonder.

"What? I was just kidding you."

"Hmmm. Well, I was driven out. I slept with one of my students. The parents found out, mother raised a stink to the Dean, and I was asked to leave."

"Wow. That's spicy," I said, really meaning that this was too much information.

"Naughty, no?" she said.

"Dangerous."

She laughed, tickled that this could be a word describing her.

"Anyway, I was open for a change. I thought I'd look for something else before I sought a position at another college."

I looked at her. She had long, brown hair, cherub

cheeks. She was wearing a flowery long summer dress. She was sweet.

"How 'bout you, Frankie! What lurks in your past?" she asked, dropping her voice to a low, bass tone. It was the first time she called me Frankie and I thought it might be the wine.

Before she drank more I thought now was as good a time as any to open the briefcase. I held up a finger, got up to retrieve the briefcase from the living room.

"There is something perhaps I've been sitting on too long," I told her. "Something serious."

She bent her head and raised her eyebrows.

"I don't know if I like serious," she said

"I know, me either. Maybe I should wait 'til another time."

"No. No, you must show me now. I'll die of curiosity."

Out with it, I thought to myself.

I opened the briefcase. I lifted the two sheets of paper laying on my laptop and placed the two photocopies before Kate.

Her jaw dropped.

"No one but a few people have seen these. Long and short of it, the police have been doing nothing since she was murdered."

Kate put her hand up to her open mouth.

"She was supposed to have committed suicide."

"So, we all heard."

I told Kate how baseball's commissioner believed she was murdered in spite of the media narrative and how my assignment shifted to helping investigate the case on the sly.

"But, how did you get these?" Kate asked.

"I'm working with a private investigator who has a source on the force."

"How was she killed?"

"You see it here. A choke collar perhaps. Maybe played a role her drowning in the sauna."

Kate spent a good moment staring at the images and shaking her head.

"Why are you showing them to me?"

I told Kate of my meeting with the police commissioner and my threat to take this evidence to the *Sun*.

"You should take them to the paper," she said.

"I have a good contact there, Rolly Singer."

"Yes, I know Rolly."

"Unless someone above him squashes it."

"Why haven't we protested to the police about them sitting on this?" she asked. "We" meaning team management.

"Good question. If I was Farley or Gazzetti, I'd be in contact with the police every day on this," I said.

Kate gazed around the room thinking, a sickening

look overcoming her face.

"You must go to Rolly. If you need to, use my name. I urge you to take these to him, Frank."

"Ok. Thank you. I needed to show these to you. Sorry to ruin the evening. Let's go into your living room and chill out."

She walked into the living room carrying her glass of wine, saying, "Any good murder mysteries you're reading, Frankie?"

We sat close to each other on the couch. A burden had been lifted from me when she urged me to reveal the photocopies to the *Sun*.

"Yes, I liked your poem about me," I said facing her. "Do you like old men?"

"Only the ones that've aged like a fine bottle of wine," she said with a sparkle in her eyes.

We heard the rumble and clap of thunder from outside. Then we heard the incessant beating of rain slashing the window panes. We got up to pull the curtain and look out a rain-streaked window to the rain bouncing on the street. Then we sat again, drank more wine, and talked about the rain.

Before long we were leaning into each other and kissing. She was a good kisser, and must have thought I was too by the way she kept kissing. Then she was leading me by the hand up the stairs and into her bedroom.

When you're young, each experience with a new girl entails learning about new body contours, new skin texture, new breath scent, etc. There are those you like more than the others and some you don't like. When you are older with all those experiences behind you, you are a little weary of what you might find, not wanting to deal with a body whose chemistry doesn't mix well with yours.

Kate was soft to the touch. Her breath from her nostrils drew me to press closer still, and her lips were desirous. I wouldn't say we made love. She might have. I'd say we had sex and thought of love as a distant possibility.

Then we lay in her bed with her head by my chest with my arm around her. We listened to the rain hard on the roof.

"Remember the play we watched?" she asked in a soft voice.

"Yes. Can't forget that too quickly."

"Remember I went over to say hello to the ball girl, Grendel?"

"Yes."

"It didn't quite hit me then like it is now."

"What do you mean?"

"Her girlfriend was wearing a chain necklace."

"I noticed."

"But it wasn't a necklace. It was choke collar. The

chain continued down her neck to her back."

"Are you sure it was choke collar?"

"The same kind of choke collar you use to make a dog heel. The same choke collar that may have been used on Greta Reich."

We were silent a good while.

"You think the ball girl could have killed her?"

"I don't know."

"I spoke to her. She had an attitude about Greta."

We listened together to the rain pouring down and the continued rumbling of thunder.

"Frank?"

"Yes?'

"I saw Gazzetti with Greta one afternoon."

"Yeah?"

"I had gone to his office suite to ask him for some direction to handle all the backlash on her. His secretary wasn't at her desk. I knocked and opened the door. He and I have a very informal relationship. He was sitting at his desk and Greta was seated on the other side of the desk. She wore a super-short dress and was crossing her legs showing them off. I noticed a bottle of wine on the desk. I told him I'd come back another time. Neither of them said a word."

"Were there wine glasses on the desk?"

"I didn't notice."

"You think Gazzetti was making a play on her?"

"That was my sense. It was an off-day. He may have called her in to celebrate her success. It's natural to celebrate with a glass of wine, no?"

"Could have been innocent enough," I replied.

"You think Gazzetti is the innocent type?"

"What do you think?"

"I'm thinking I think what you think."

"You think Gazzetti could have killed Greta?"

"Wouldn't he have to have had a motive?"

"Maybe Gazzetti is a psycho?"

"He looks the part."

We stayed quiet. Then we slept, the rain on the roof the lullaby that put us out.

Chapter 32

Kate drove me back to the hotel in the morning. While showering I thought how I should approach Rolly Singer. It was Sunday, and the Club was playing the last game of the homestand this afternoon. I wasn't sure I could find a private place with him at the ballpark. In the morning, he might be flying to Miami to cover the games against the Marlins. I decided to call and ask him to come to my hotel room.

Rolly knocked on my door at eleven. He walked in sporting red suspenders over a white short-sleeved shirt. He'd developed a considerable paunch since my days covering sports for the *Reporter* and his hair had grayed and thinned.

"I hope this is good," he said stepping by me. "Can you keep this to twenty minutes?"

I wasted no time in laying out the two photocopies showing Greta's corpse in the sauna. Singer brought out his glasses to view them. He leaned over the table shifting his head side to side. "Who is this?"

If you had never seen Greta nude before or her pro-filed face jammed against the bottom of a tub, her hair wet and slick, or her lying down looking as pale as a fog at dawn, you probably would not identify her in these images.

"Greta Reich."

"Where'd you get these?"

"I have a source inside police headquarters. Only a few people have ever seen them."

I told Rolly of my meeting with the police commis-sioner.

"You want me to get the *Sun* to publish them. I don't know if I can do that."

"Would the *Sun* rather these images go viral on so-cial media, or my old paper scoops it?" I still had contacts at the *Reporter*, but the *Sun* still had the greatest reader-ship and clout. Besides, my long friendship with Singer was based on mutual respect and affinity, and was tight-er than any relationship I had with writers still with the *Reporter*. The most loyal move would have been to my old paper, perhaps; but in the best interest of Greta's legacy, I went to the *Sun*.

"If you haven't noticed, our editor these days is Wil-ma Tegren. She's a staunch feminist. I know she couldn't stand Miss Reich. I heard her rant against her myself. You're right, these people want to push the narrative she killed herself. Having her murdered would do more to prop her legend. Son of a bitch." Rolly turned to smile my way. "Don't worry, old friend, I'm not going to stand down to Tegren. I'll present these in such a way she won't be able to sit on them, I don't think."

"Not worried she'll fire you?"

"She's been threatening to retire me the last two years. I'd welcome it."

No sooner had Singer left with the copies in a manila envelope, I got a call from Buffalo Bob.

"Jeez!" he exclaimed, "I almost got shot squeezing that dork!"

After another dramatic proclamation, I got him to tell me what happened, blow by blow.

He had confronted Rene Corcoran, the trainer, over the timeline of his arrival at the ballpark that fateful day and all he had seen. Then Corcoran, agitated by Bob, had security called into the clubhouse. The security guard noticed a bulge in Bob's front pocket and asked Bob what it was. Bob did not answer the question but rather started reaching his right hand into his pocket. Slowly Bob continued reaching down in. The guard pulled his gun and shouted for Bob to halt. But Bob, risking being downed right there, ever so slowly, hesitatingly, pulled out what was making the pants pocket bulge.

It was a can of mace.

"Friggin guard was ready to pop me over a can of mace."

"You could have just told him what it was. Sounds like you created the suspense."

"Yeah, well, he's an idiot."

I wanted to say you're the idiot but didn't want to insult the man who was partnering with me still.

"It may have been Morton," Bob said.

"Morton, what?"

"Morton who killed her."

"Why do you say that, Bob?" I asked, rolling my eyes with the cell phone to my ear.

"Corcoran saw him leaving Eutaw Street when he was coming in."

"That's all you got?" I said, though it was something to look into. "What did Corcoran say?"

"He was walking past the Babe Ruth statue and he heard this long whistle. He looked up and saw Morton looking at his Rottweiler running toward him."

"Is that all Corcoran said he saw?"

"Yeah. Look I don't buy Morton's Buddhism crap. You can't be a pacifist and catch major league pitching. You can't be a wuss. My gut says he's the killer."

"You did good, Bob."

"Thanks, I think we've nailed him."

"I mean, you did good in staring down Barney Fife."

Buffalo Bob laughed. "Yeah, he was a Barney Fife, you got that right."

I felt obligated to see the game and return to the clubhouse after it, since it was the last chance I'd have in a couple weeks to talk with the players unless I traveled with the team. Baltimore lost the game, shut out by the Tigers' ace starter. The clubhouse atmosphere was as friendly as can be after a loss and the team is struggling to play .500 ball. Players kept the joking and razzing way down, but not totally out. I'd see one player flick a towel at another one's butt, and another player pranking the one in the locker next to him applying glue to where he would sit.

I shuffled around, small-talking with those that seemed approachable. Riobonito, the second baseman, was dressing quietly at his locker. We had met when Greta motorcycled us over to his house. "You miss her presence?" I asked him when we had exchanged nods.

He didn't immediately answer, but then looked at me with a sad, small smile. He was one of the players who had connected with her.

I went back down the hall toward Ralston's office, noting that the door to the ball girls' locker room was shut. I hesitated, but went on by. The manager saw me outside the window looking into his office and waved me in. He was sitting in his desk chair chewing a wad of tobacco and shooting brown juice through his lips into a spittoon on the floor, something I hadn't seen in a while and only out west in old bars.

"Better luck in Miami, skipper," I told him. "I'll be going back to my home to work on my book, unless something new breaks. I do have one question for you before I go: How did Greta and Morton get along during a game? How was she with his pitch calls?"

Ralston grunted. "The little squirt shook his calls more than a rookie might or should. Wally went to the mound more than once and chewed her out. A fan wouldn't have noticed it. Wally smiled to camouflage that he was pissed. He'd walk with a halting motion."

I left the park to go over to the cigar club east of my hotel. Sitting in its outdoor patio, with tobacco smoke floating before me and its flavor in my palate, I wondered if and when Rolly Singer would call a meeting on the photocopied image.

I found my answer the next morning.

When I opened the door to my room to reach down for the paper, the headlines looked triumphant: "MURDER CLOUD RISES OVER REICH'S GRAVE. Leaked Images Leave Suicide Narrative in Doubt." The images were plastered on page two.

Chapter 33

Singer and the managing editor had driven the images to Wilma Tegren's house in Towson on Sunday afternoon after the game. They double-teamed her and were persuasive that the images had to run in Monday's paper. Initially, according to Singer, she fought it; but when the *Sun's* editor saw how adamant her famed writer and managing editor were that the story run, she caved.

The fallout throughout mainstream and social media was swift and extensive. It was like the day after her death all over again. Those that hated Greta clung to the suicide angle, coming up with absurd reasoning of how she killed herself, given the new images. Those who had loved Greta's talent and spunk voiced outrage over the police chief's inaction.

I got a call from Buffalo Bob before noon. The chief had called a meeting first thing in response to the *Sun's* coverage. His brother Tom had been unleashed onto the case. "The killer's shakin' in his boots this morning, you can bet," said Bob.

Right after his call the William Tell Overture played again on my phone. I liked to fantasize I was a man of action. It was Commissioner Antonelli.

"I saw the story in the *Sun* on the Internet. Things are moving fast, it seems. Fill me in."

I told Antonelli about how the images were leaked and how I brought them to Singer.

"We're moving too fast," he said, sounding a little exasperated. "I didn't want this angle to spin out of control. This not only puts pressure on the chief, but on the ballclub, and on me. Farley and the rest of the owners won't be happy about this development."

"I understand," I told him.

"Baseball has to move forward. We can't be mired in scandal. We're always looking forward. Teams are meeting with their scouts for plans to sign their top prospects. GMs are dealing with the trading deadline this week. I wanted an investigation under the radar."

I was silent. I was more than happy with this development. I had forgotten for the moment how Antonelli had wanted a clandestine investigation. He chastised me with his next comment.

"This time you keep me informed," he said. "I want to know who's being investigated. Keep close. Keep me informed."

I figured I had gotten the commissioner's raw reaction to the news, upsetting his intentions, so I didn't judge his reaction. I followed his call with a call to Kate.

"Yes, I saw it," Kate said. "Rolly delivered. You feel better?"

'Yes. Maybe now we'll get some action. By the way, I understand Gazzetti may be meeting with the team's scouts in the field. Know anything about that?"

"I do. I've got a press release on it ready to go out. Gazzetti is meeting with each one over the next three days."

Events began overtaking the normal pace of things. The next morning the *Sun* front page headlines took me by surprise: "MAYOR FIRES POLICE CHIEF. Unhappy with Strauss's Handling of Reich Investigation."

It was a good move by a corrupt mayor, covering up her own incompetence by getting rid of the police chief for the incompetence she aided and abetted in. She would look good by acting fast. According to the article she promoted the man below him to fill the top spot. He was a decorated Iraq war veteran which gave good optics to a fresh start. She ordered him to do "due diligence" in the Reich investigation. I just hoped I wouldn't have reason to approach him as I had his predecessor.

I was starting to feel things might be breaking in a logical manner.

That afternoon I met with the scout, Pete Sake, at the Lord Baltimore's lobby bar. At three in the afternoon it would give us the privacy needed for the questions I intended to ask. I told him I'd buy him a drink if he'd give me a little more time to fill in some blanks for my book.

Lord Baltimore had an old classic lobby where guests lounged and drank cocktails not far from the front desk. The bar in the far corner away from it all had no one sitting at it when we met.

Sake ordered a Jack Daniels straight up and I did too to seem friendly. Sake was a tall man, and his height commanded the bar.

I started in with small talk, asking if he had any promising prospects he was looking to bring under contract. He said he had two pitchers he was hoping to sign, pending the go-ahead from Gazzetti, who he was meeting with tomorrow. I saw an easy segue to Greta.

"Either of them have the assortment of pitches Greta had?" I asked, nonchalant.

"No, they got speed and a slider. They'll develop more in time. More than anything it was her ability to throw at various speeds that made her effective."

"She ever mix it up with you?"

"Don't follow ya."

"Ever feel she was inviting you in, only to change speed?"

"Not sure what you're getting at," he said in his southern drawl.

"She was a big tease. You find her that way in Colombia?"

Sake sipped his Jack Daniels a few times without a word. I thought he was going to clam up.

"Ever get close to her?"

"The guy you may want to ask is the man who brought her up," he said eyeing me.

I gave him the look I wasn't following him.

"The GM, man."

"Gazzetti?"

"He came down and gave her a good look over. I mean from head to toe."

"Are you saying Gazzetti made a move on her?'

"Oh, I'm not gonna say one way or another. What I saw. No. Hey, you got to know her. You can figure it out. You think a big league GM is going to bet his career on a little girl who throws no faster than a junk baller? There's gotta be some testosterone driving that gamble."

While my thoughts were running down that rabbit hole, Sake downed the rest of his Jack Daniels and got up. "Thanks for the drink, Barr. Gotta be somewhere. Good luck." He walked through the lobby past the front desk and out the front door.

I never got to ask him if he had forced himself on her. What would it matter now anyway? The accusation of rape was dead and buried. I thought of Gazzetti, remembering what Kate told me she saw in his office.

Chapter 34

Buffalo Bob, his brother Tom, and myself met again in the row house, upstairs at the kitchen table on a Thursday afternoon, the Baseball Club still away. I noticed binoculars on the table as I was mindful not to sit in his father's chair. Bob was brewing coffee as we waited for his brother to show.

"You know, Frank, most people can't put two and two together," Bob said, handing me a cup of the coffee he brewed.

"You're probably right about that. If most people could the world would work better."

"Amen."

I was waiting to see if Bob would circle around to a greater point, maybe some news on the case, when we heard the front door's buzzer. Bob went down to the first floor to open the door for his brother who bounded up the stairs.

"Things are moving, Frank. There are two of us on the case," Tom said. "I questioned several who work in the clubhouse. There are some leads to people I need to get to. But we're moving. I figure you played no small role there."

"How's the new chief on this?" I asked Tom.

"I've known McMullen for twenty years. He's with us. We'll get this killer."

"I have a beat on him," said Bob.

"How's that, Bob?" his brother asked.

"I staked out the suspect Sunday. I believe it's him."

Tom looked at me, bemused.

"Who Bob?"

"But you have to put two and two together to see it," Bob said.

"Bob, what have you been up to?"

"See these binoculars?"

"Yes, I see them."

"They know who the killer is."

"All right, Bob. Stop talking in riddles. Tell us what you have."

"I staked out Monk Morton's home on Gittings Street by the Rowhouse Grill on Sunday."

"That was a gameday," I noted out loud.

"I was there early in the morning."

"Where'd you plant?" Tom asked him.

Right up the street, waiting for him to come out for breakfast. He's a bachelor. I figured he'd be out for one of the breakfast joints in the neighborhood."

"Did he come out."

"He came out and with his Rottweiler."

"Okay, where'd he go?"

"I tailed him. He took his dog for a walk up to Federal Hill Park. It's nice up there. I had my binoculars on him the whole time."

"Trying to be inconspicuous, were you?" Tom asked his brother.

"We got him."

"We got him?"

"You put two and two together and we got him."

"What am I missing?" Tom asked.

I sat by wondering what Buffalo Bob was driving toward. If nothing else he had us totally captivated.

"The dog collar. The choke chain. He walked his Rottweiler heeling by him the whole walk on a choke chain."

"Bob, are you linking Morton to the murder because he walks his dog with a choke chain?"

"No, I'm linking Morton to the murder because he didn't walk his dog with a choke chain."

"Bob, you're not making any sense," Tom chided his brother. "Look, I'm working with you on this one, but I need you to deal in reality."

In that last remark, I sensed there was an intense history regarding Bob's grip on the real world.

On the other hand, I saw what Bob was saying. "Monk Morton was seen walking on the Eutaw Street concourse away out of the Park the afternoon she was killed," I said, according to what Bob dug up. "His dog wasn't on a leash."

Buffalo Bob shifted his eyes back and forth from me to his brother like laser beams.

"You gotta put two and two together," he said.

Tom looked at his brother trying to do just that.

He dragged as much detail he could out of Bob as to what the trainer, Rene Corcoran, had seen.

I told them Monk Morton had been closer to Greta than any other player. It was hard to imagine him being the killer. He would have to be psychologically profiled. Remarks by Greta and Ralston suggested he had a controlling personality. That's all I knew of him.

"I'll try to get a search warrant," Tom said. "Maybe the judge will grant it on this story."

Tom rose to leave and started walking toward the staircase. He paused to look back to the table where the binoculars stood, and shook his head, smiling.

Chapter 35

I went over to Kate's house that night, anxious to share some of the news about the investigation, yet feeling ambivalent about going there. We might be on the scent of the killer but somehow, in going to Kate's place, I didn't feel I was doing right by Greta's memory. I was playing a role in looking for who did it to get justice for Greta, but, at the same time I was already in bed with another woman, looking forward to being in that bed again. This would not have happened if Greta was alive. At least I told myself that. But the sex drive has no morality. Someone who grieves doesn't seek company as quickly as this.

Maybe, I thought to myself, Greta only fed an animal's lust for life. Making me feel young again and full of desire was what she had offered. It's quite a trip back being nineteen again.

A meal cooking in the kitchen wafted all the way forward to the living room where I sat again reading one of Kate's books. I was reading a short story by Harry Mark

Petrakis, who became known for his novel, *A Dream of Kings*. The short story I was reading was full of the mystery of life and one man's passion for it. Greta had that passion. Kate had it too, maybe with more self-awareness than young Greta.

I was so musing when Kate called me into the kitchen for dinner. I shut the book and laid it down. She had prepared a lasagna. Half way through it she disclosed it was all vegetarian and non-dairy. What I assumed was ricotta cheese was made from cashew nuts. There were no pasta strips in it. Zucchini strips were substituted.

"You are amazing," I complimented her, hoping to see her smile and blush, which she did.

I made Kate promise confidentiality in what I would disclose and told her of the various developments.

On the latest, she offered some insight of her own.

"If Morton killed her, it was likely a spur of the moment thing. Deep down he harbored hate for Greta. He saw an opportunity and just like that, acted on it," Kate speculated. "If he did it, it was one reckless act. He used his dog collar and left it there as evidence or ditched it. I know most criminals are stupid but this really takes the cake. No, I don't buy it."

"Well, don't tell that to Buffalo Bob. He's on a high right now, thinking he's on the right scent."

"What do you think?" she asked me.

As she asked I wondered if Greta had asked me things in conversation. I wondered if we had had much conversation outside the interviews for the book.

"I think maybe he was obsessed with her. He found her so desirable but couldn't control her. He's a controller. A catcher tries to control a baseball game. He and the pitcher are the two players who feel close to being able to control a game's outcome. But Monk couldn't control Greta. She had her own mind what she wanted to throw a batter. She was constantly shaking him off."

"You have to be more than a control freak to kill someone, don't you think?"

"Are English teachers always this smart?"

"I'm not smart. Just curious."

After dinner, she led me into her bedroom for what she promised was dessert. There was a distinct difference in the sex I had encountered with Greta, which centered on her skin and her loins, and the sex Kate ambushed me with, centering on my skin and loins. Greta was all about receiving pleasure, and I hungrily gave her that. Kate was all about giving me pleasure. I wouldn't deny her.

Chapter 36

The phone rang in the middle of the night waking us both. Kate reached over to the end table by her bedside for her cell. She then handed me the phone, feigning an overjoyed smile. "It's Buffalo Bob."

"Frank, come on over to 2510 Charles Street."

"What's going on? Can't wait till morning?"

"Grendel Forrest just been arrested for assaulting her girlfriend. The place looks like a tornado hit it."

"Do you really need me there?" I asked, groggy from a beautiful slumber interrupted.

"You gotta look at her room. The photos on the wall. We can get you in."

The way he put it, I was part of the team after all. Dutifully I sat up and got dressed. Kate was propped up on her side, her head up and resting on her hand.

"I'll be back. Sooner or later. But I'll be back."

It was one in the morning. I got in my car two blocks away and drove west through Harbor neighborhoods and past the Inner Harbor, wondering how Buffalo Bob had known I was with Kate. It was a mystery in and of itself. I took a right on Charles. With little traffic at this hour I was at the 2500 block in ten minutes time.

Three police cruisers lined the street, double-parked in front of 2510, a three-story brick building with officers walking in and out the front door. Buffalo Bob came out as I walked back after parking my car. The police were familiar with him, knew he was Tom's brother and was on the case with Tom. Bob led me into the building and up a stairwell to a second-floor flat. The place looked like a brawl had taken place. A couple chairs were sideways on the floor. A sofa cushion was on the floor resting against the sofa with a foot-long gash exposing foam strips. A photograph of Grendel, the ball girl, down the left field line in foul territory was on the ground, its glass cracked.

"Come in here," Bob said. I followed him into a bedroom.

On the wide wall were the photos. All were Greta. Greta pitching, as seen from the left field line. Greta with puckered lips and a bath towel wrapped around her, one hand raising some towel to show off more thigh. There were several photos of Greta in short dresses in different places. One shot looked up at her backside as she rode an escalator, which might have been at the Galleria Mall. More shots show Greta shopping at stores in the Mall. It didn't look like Greta knew she was being photographed.

There was not one photograph that was disturbing. What was disturbing were all the photographs on the wall of Grendel's bedroom.

Tom Grazer came into the room. He looked at the wall and to me said, "Yes, this makes her a suspect, all right. That and the nature of the assault." He walked back out of the room.

Bob reported what he knew of what happened.

"Her girlfriend went postal on her. The cops got here and they were facing off screaming at each other. She's at the station now pressing charges against Grendel for assault. Seems Grendel was choking her to death. It was a nightly ritual. I guess she'd had enough of it. She turned on Grendel and came at her with a butcher knife."

Tom came back in and sidled up to me. "The judge nixed the warrant. I'll be paying a visit to the Monk next week when the team is back in town. Meanwhile I just got a call from the station where they took both of them. Laurie, the girl friend, is fingering Grendel for Reich's murder. They both will be going into the interrogation room."

"I've spoken to Grendel. She had an attitude about Greta Reich. A rancor."

"I'm going there now. You can observe if you like."

I took Tom up on the offer and drove to the auxiliary police station on Tremont Street, meeting both Tom and

Bob there.

Chapter 37

Tom led us down a corridor and into a small room with a window that saw into a bare room with a table and a chair on each side of it. A microphone was on the table. Within five minutes Laurie Englewood was led into the room by an officer who shut the door behind her. She was the same blond Kate and I saw at the theater bar during the Irish wake performance. She looked distressed, her hair mussed. Two minutes later a detective Ted Goner walked in, short and muscular. He looked like he lifted weights day and night at a gym. He wore a light green, short-sleeve dress shirt with a Kelly-green tie loosened around the collar.

I told Tom Kate and I had seen her at the play and Kate had noticed her neck jewelry was actually a choke collar. Tom listened, inclining his head slightly toward me as he watched through the window where Detective Goner was talking to Englewood.

After some basic questioning to establish her identity and relationship to Grendel Forrest, the blond girl started sobbing and covering her face with her hand. Suddenly she placed outstretched arms onto the table, her hands making a fist, and screamed, "She was torturing me! There was never a day she didn't near kill me. Choking me!"

"Tell me about it. When would she choke you. How?"

"She made me wear the dog collar. It was a choke chain, you know," she said, bringing a hand to her throat and fingering it gently.

"I had to wear it all the time."

"You had to wear it?"

"If I didn't wear it she was cold to me. So I wore it, you know, for her affection. I know it's stupid. And she'd be sweet one moment and the next moment she'd be pulling on the chain so hard that I'd whimper. It would cut off my air. Sometimes I'd almost pass out. She loved to hear me whimper.

"Like a dog she'd walk me around, making me heel. She'd reward me with a dog bone. You know, a Milk Bone."

Laurie was looking straight at Goner. "Yes! I ate doggie treats! That's how sick it is!"

Goner waited for her to calm and then spoke. "The officers who arrived at the scene say you had a Bowie knife raised in your hand. I have to ask, did you attack Grendel with the intent to harm her?'

Laurie looked at Goner in disbelief and disgust. She

leaned her neck forward, clutching it with one hand where the choke chain had done its work. She pleaded, "She was killing me. She took away who I was. Whoever I was."

She sat back now and just stared at the detective.

"Who owns the Bowie knife?" Goner asked.

"Grendel brought it home one day." The detective waited. "She liked to tease me with it. You know, run the cold blade over my skin, get me aroused with fear."

Goner said nothing for a good minute.

"Do you feel you raised the knife with an intent to kill your abuser?"

Laurie shot up out of the chair, her arm outstretched pointing to the door.

"She's the killer! She killed Greta Reich! I know she did."

"Tell me what you know," Goner said.

"She was obsessed with her. She stalked her. She took photos of her and plastered them on our goddamn bedroom wall. She would humiliate me telling how much she wanted Greta."

"Go on."

"She'd leash me and have me sit on the floor like a dog sits, while she sat on the bed masturbating, looking at the photos of her. Then she'd ask me how hot I thought Greta was and she'd choke me until I was panting, looking at her photos.

"You know, I didn't mind her games. But then she started telling me how pathetic a girl I was and how Greta was so hot, so smart. She'd say how she'd like to get it on with her and then say I wasn't desirable in bed." Laurie wiped her eyes with her bare hands. A moist film barely held back a new wave of tears. "She hurt me."

"How do you know she killed Greta Reich?"

Laurie was flabbergasted. "Isn't it obvious! The photos in the papers. Grendel's locker room was just down the hall. What do you guys need?"

"A motive, for one," said Goner.

"Motive? She hated Greta."

"You spoke about how much she desired her."

"Greta spurned her! Grendel bought her a gorgeous set of earrings, she was so sweet on her, and Greta said she couldn't accept them and was cool to her from then on. Grendel desired her but couldn't have her. So, she hated her."

Goner sat quietly for a moment, then said, "Where were you that Saturday afternoon Greta Reich was killed?"

Lauri stared at Goner and then averted her eyes to the wall. Goner repeated the question.

"I'm not sure," she said. "Maybe I was out, maybe I was home."

"Think back. Take your time."

"I don't recall exactly."

"Do you know where Greta was that afternoon?"

"I don't know. Maybe she was with me."

At that juncture, another officer opened the door and called Goner out of the room. Goner than came back in and told Laurie she was free to go. Grendel was refusing to press charges.

"We may want to question you further regarding Greta Reich. But you can go now. Unless, maybe you wish to press charges against your roommate."

She looked at Goner with a blank stare taking in what had just been told her. After a good moment she said, "Thank you, detective. not at this time."

Just like that, after accusing her girlfriend of cruelty and murder, she could not bring herself to press charges. I had no doubt the two would share their bed again tonight. I supposed the choke collar and Bowie knife would be used once again as a measure of the love between them.

In a matter of minutes Grendel replaced Laurie in the interrogation room. Tom left us and appeared at the table opposite her.

Chapter 38

Grendel sat with her arms folded gripping both shoulders, hugging herself and smiling pleasantly.

"What's it like being a ball girl for the Baseball Club? Your second year now, no?" Tom asked her after introducing himself.

"That's right."

"And your day job is with Exact Home Improvement in Baltimore, I understand. What do you do there?"

"Customer service, mainly help people find what they're looking for in the aisles. If the item is high up I'll retrieve it for them."

"How did you come to be the team's ball girl?"

Grendel became loquacious. She told of how she met second baseman Juan Riobonito at a bar, that when he heard she played softball in a city league, he suggested she apply to be a ball girl. She did, and Riobonito put in a good word for her.

"Juan is a sweet man. I love being a ball girl."

"What did you think, you had a ringside seat, when

Greta Reich pitched her first game at the ball park that Sunday afternoon?"

"I thought, wow, this girl is doing it. I couldn't believe her. Her size. Her slight build. But she had strong legs. You need that to pitch."

"She liked showing off those legs, didn't she?"

"I suppose so. She loved those short dresses. She put a slit up her pants. Yeah, she was a show-off."

"It must have hurt when she refused to take the earrings you gave her."

Grendel stopped being talkative. She looked around the room and up at the window we were looking through., Goner, Bob and myself could see her but she could only see the glass reflecting Tom and her.

"Am I being charged with something here?"

"What do you know about the murder of Greta Reich?"

"Just what everybody knows, I guess."

"Not everybody was obsessed with her."

"Are you referring to the photos in the bedroom?"

"Judging by those pictures, you were stalking her. How often did you follow her?"

"I just saw her on a couple occasions while I was walking by the Harbor. I took some pictures. It was spur of the moment."

"When did you arrive at the ballpark the day of her

murder?"

It struck me how Tom was forthright in his method of questioning where his brother prevaricated in conversation. Bob, standing to my left, just then commented, "I'd chip away at the blonde angle. She likes blondes." I would have enjoyed Buffalo Bob playing cat and mouse interrogating her.

"I got to the ballpark a few hours later, I guess," Grendel replied. "Hey, what is this? You think I had anything to do with her death?"

"You and the killer enjoy using a choke chain on a girl's neck."

"Look, I wasn't there."

Tom was silent, waiting for Grendel to spill something, anything.

"You get pleasure in treating your girlfriend like a dog?"

When she had walked into the room her demeanor was matronly but friendly, cloaking the bully inside her with smiles and the warmth of being hugged, albeit by her own arms. Now her smiles disappeared and her arms rested on her thighs, tensed like a wrestler waiting for the opponent to charge in.

"Did Laurie press charges, or anything?" Grendel asked.

"Not as of yet."

"Well, if you don't mind, I'm tired. I'll be happy to answer any questions, but I'm going home now."

"Keep that choke chain off her neck," Tom said, calmly.

"It's only role play, detective. Consenting adults. It's our way of showing affection."

Grendel got up and walked out with a trace of swagger. Tom did nothing to detain her.

Chapter 39

I was sitting on a bench in Washington Park, City Hall to my right, police headquarters behind me. I was waiting for Buffalo Bob to show. After a while I pulled out a cigar from the breast pocket on my shirt, pulled out a cutter from my pants pocket and snipped the tapered end of the torpedo. I sat there in the warm afternoon breeze sniffing the outer tobacco leaves that were wrapped tight. I saw Bob turn the corner and wheeling toward me on his retro bike.

"What's up?" I asked him as he jostled the kickstand with his foot. He wore a Baltimore Ravens jersey and plaid, short pants that fell just below the knees. He sat down beside me.

"Where's your Baseball Club jersey?" I chided him good naturedly.

'I don't watch them," he said.

"I thought everyone in this city was a fan."

"Well, don't tell anyone," he said, concern on his face that I might turn him in. "TV killed that game."

I looked at him, wondering if had read my book. I agreed with his statement.

"Wrong game for TV," he said.

"How's that?"

"All the action runs on predictable straight lines."

I just looked at him, figuring he'd continue on this tract.

"You know. Batter runs in a straight line to first, then to second, and so forth. An outfielder runs in a straight line to get to a ball. A pitcher throws the ball in a straight line to the plate. Curve balls are pretty much imperceptible."

"Hmmm." I was finding Bob to be fascinating.

"Now, football. That's a sport made for TV. All zigzag action. Much more titillating to the senses. Football to the eye is unpredictable like jazz is to the ear."

"I'm mentally taking notes. Just to warn you now, I may use this."

"We wanted to fill you in on the latest developments," he said in an instant 180.

"What do we have?" This question apparently triggered a humorous notion inside his head.

"Well," he said, giggling. "We don't –" and the giggling turned into laughter and he couldn't turn that spigot off. "We don't have –" And he laughed on. "Oh geez, ho." He tried to get it under control. "We don't –" and the laughter shot up like a geyser, with Bob leaning back on the bench, his hand covering his convulsing face. He proved again to be his own best comic audience with the lines never having to be delivered.

"Bob," I repeated. "What do we have?"

Bob stopped laughing and looked at me unsurely, then looked left and right and behind him.

"We should wait for Tom. He's in with the police chief now."

"Okay. Want a cigar?" I took the second cigar in my pocket and offered it to him. I always carried two cigars just for this purpose.

"Well geez, thanks." He took the cigar and looked it over with uncertainty about what do with it. I took it back, snipped the end, and took out a small box of wooden matches. There was hardly a breeze that would snuff out a flame. I struck a match and lit the cigar I'd put in between my lips and nodded to Bob to follow suit.

Bob looked surreptitiously to his left and right again, and then glanced over his back, like a kid afraid his mother might be watching.

"You ever smoke a cigar?"

"Uh, well, I'm not sure." He put it in his mouth and I lit the end. Bob had no sooner began to puff on it before he began to cough from the harsh smoke.

I gave him a quick lesson on how to draw the smoke

into the palate without inhaling and blowing the smoke out. He tried again and threw a fit to the point it seemed his limbs might fly off his body.

"Slow, Bob. You're puffing too quick and sucking in too hard. Relax."

Pretty soon he was getting the hang of it.

"Not bad," he said.

"So, Bob, any new evidence?" I asked, anxious to hear something about the case.

"Well, alright, I guess I can tell you."

"Go ahead."

"Grendel wasn't working that day of the murder."

I digested this important piece of information, wondering if Tom Grazer and the DA was making a move on her.

"But she has an alibi," Bob added. "Seems she was with Laurie Englewood that afternoon playing their S&M games."

"That's the alibi? How credible does Tom think that is?"

"If you think about it, it's pretty credible," Bob said, exuding a sense of logic.

"There were no marks on her either," Bob added.

"What do you mean?" I asked.

"Like there were no marks on Gazzetti."

"Gazzetti? What are you talking about, Bob?" He was

being his obscure self once again. I prodded him to make sense.

"Gazzetti handled her but there were no marks on him."

"What the hell are you talking about?"

"Wait a second, you don't know it was Gazzetti that pulled her out of the sauna?"

I was completely baffled once again by Buffalo Bob. My expression must have shown this.

"Well, I didn't know this myself until I was with Tom at the station that night and you had left. They wanted to keep a lid on this until there was further investigation."

"Keep a lid on what?"

Bob again looked around him with furtive eyes and a dramatic grimace.

"It was Gazzetti who found her. He had gone down to the clubhouse to talk with her. Says he knocked on her door, opened it a bit and called in, but got no answer. He went into the room and found her submerged. He lifted her out of the sauna and onto the massage table and tried mouth to mouth on her. Five minutes, he said, before he called out for help."

I was dumbfounded.

At that moment Tom Grazer was walking toward us.

"Glad you could make it," he said, shaking my hand. "Since when do you smoke cigars?" he asked his brother.

"First time. Frank here's a bad influence."

Tom smiled looking at us.

"I was just hearing for the first time that it was Gazzetti who found Greta in the sauna," I said.

Tom frowned and looked at Bob accusingly. "We don't want that leaked to the press. It won't help anything."

"Have you grilled Gazzetti about it?"

"Sure. We think he's on the up and up."

"Besides," said Bob, "Gazzetti has an alibi."

I took that comment in and threw back the obvious question. "What alibi?"

"He found her after she was murdered and tried to save her," said Bob, dead serious. His brother Tom wore a broad smile.

"Sure," said Tom, "The GM is person of interest, naturally. But the investigation has to search beyond the moment she was found."

"And Grendel?" I asked.

"Her alibi is credible in theory. Says she was with her girlfriend all afternoon. Her girlfriend backs this up. We're looking for more evidence."

"Tom, her girlfriend believed Grendel had killed Greta. Why'd she say that? For revenge? Which story is true?"

"Frank, in my business it pays to read more into a

person's actions than her words. That Laurie went back to her apartment to sleep again with Grendel speaks volumes."

"And Grendel, the fact that she stalked Greta, taking photos of her, what does that say?"

"Keep following the story line. She took the photos, put them on the wall, so she could humiliate her submissive partner and get off on it."

I thought about that. Tom might be making sense.

"What about Monk Morton. Did you speak with him?" I asked.

"He says he did walk his dog around the park with his leash off, but had kept the choke collar on his dog."

"Do you believe him."

"I don't believe anybody," Tom said, eyeing me shrewdly.

"But you believe Gazzetti?" I said.

"I don't disbelieve him right now. That jury is still out."

There was still legwork to be done in several directions, Tom told me before looking at his watch and then returning to the police building behind him.

Bob got up from the bench then and went over to straddle his bike. He put the bike helmet on his head and snapped the strap. He started peddling by me, then dropped one foot to the ground, turning to me. "It's why

I like riding this bike," he said, "I can zigzag."

He rode away, zigzagging through the small city park and soon onto the street and then leaning to turn around the corner. I began to think that he was prolonging his boyhood by an intelligent design I was not able to fathom.

Chapter 40

I had time to kill before I would have dinner with Kate Bower. I had never seen the Babe Ruth Museum. All the years I covered baseball for the *Reporter* and I never went to it, feeling I would wait until I had a son to take with me. With that plan never in the works, I still stayed away, probably feeling guilty I wasn't a dad. How can one ever measure up to his father without that adult rite of passage?

Somehow I shirked the guilt that afternoon, feeling that die had been cast. The museum was set up in the stoop house the Babe grew up in. I found it near Camden Yards. The Babe was always a marvel to watch. Growing up, decades after he was gone, baseball lore and literature portrayed him as a God, with powers supernatural. How else could a clownish man with a beer belly well surpass every other player in hitting home runs by a huge margin?

Roger Maris in 1961 needed eight more games added to the season to surpass Ruth by one homer. Mark

McGuire and Barry Bonds needed steroids to pass him. Ruth's legacy only shined greater with the backdrop of these shenanigans. I went to the museum looking for a spark of inspiration for my writing on baseball, even the one in the note stage on Greta.

I walked down a hallway on a hardwood floor between brick walls and curiously, into a room that celebrated the old Baltimore Colts and famed quarterback, Johnny Unitas. I had not expected to find this. I looked at black and white photos of Unitas and others on the wall and then watched a video on a wall screen.

Unitas was my favorite football player growing up. No one to this day had a grit or style like his. I loved the way he threw long passes in a high arc that fell beyond the reach of defenders and into the arms of Colt receivers. I also loved his sleight of hand, seemingly handing off the ball to one running back and then to another, sometimes keeping the ball hidden to drop back and throw it. One play on the screen had me following one runner only to find the halfback with the ball running at the top of the screen, fooling even the cameraman.

The inclusion of the Colts and Unitas on the museum floor had been a welcome surprise, getting my mind off the tragedy and the progress of the investigation. I walked back to the Waterfront, showered and changed, and took a cab to Kate's row house in the Canton neighborhood.

At this juncture I was not smitten with Kate, but certainly charmed by her. She loved to laugh and cook, read and talk. We both enjoyed poetry. I fit into her space well for a few hours at a time. She seemed to be keen on me and this was a parachute I needed during my free fall when Greta was killed.

While we were eating dinner at her kitchen table, a garlic pie she called it, she asked me a lot of questions about growing up. I told her I had played a lot of football and basketball, a little baseball, and she started talking about how she was a majorette and would march down the football field leading her high school band. My mind, as was its proclivity, drifted from the talk and was marching back to the Unitas clips I had watched and some sensation, a feeling of untold prescience I had when watching it, something even at this moment I couldn't put a finger on.

Later, Kate led me back into her bedroom and I wondered what it might be like, two people having digested a lot of garlic. The odor coming out of our pores seemed to compliment the adhesion of our bodies in the lovemaking. It stood out more as we lay in bed, sleeping on and off through the night. I think it was the smell of garlic from her nostrils that woke me from the one dream that gave me the revelation.

The scene that stuck with me after I woke had me carrying a football and then stretching on the ground, and somehow Greta was squirming naked near me, being dragged by a chain, the arm pulling her clothed in a suit cloth, the hand yanking her by a choke chain, and the wrist reflecting a glint of sunlight. I placed my hands behind my head on the pillow, the revelation hitting me.

Maybe it wasn't Pete Sake who raped Greta. Maybe it was really Gazzetti and Greta couldn't face that she was captive to the man who brought her to the major leagues. Greta wouldn't go to the police about Sake because she was feigning with him as the predator for the need to share with me the trauma of being raped. But it was Gazzetti all along.

When she left my room that fateful day to go early to the ball park she said she was going to stand up to Gazzetti. I assumed she was going to make her case why he should keep her on the team in spite of all the upheaval of horrible publicity surrounding her. Maybe she went to threaten him to lay off her, not subjugate her any more with cruel sadistic play. After all, she was no stranger to the press and may well have flashed that card before Gazzetti. Maybe Gazzetti fumed after she walked out of his office and then went down to her private locker to teach her another lesson of who he was. I can see him throwing a choke chain on her neck and leading her around the room naked, being over aggressive, getting carried away with the perverse thrill of yanking on the chain until he went too far. Keeping a cool head, he came up with a plan to save himself. He placed her in the sauna and filled it with water, waited a few minutes and drained the tub, took that picture of her face on the drain, then pulled her out and lay her on the massage table and went through the motions of mouth-to-mouth resuscitation. He was hands-on with the players and could very well have known that Grendel's girlfriend wore the choke chain, and, I later learned, one of his players. He gambled the one he used on Greta would not be traced to him.

I kept this revelation inside and shared it with no one. It needed time to take root in a logic beyond the senses contained in slumber. It wouldn't be the last time I put too much stock in a dream.

Chapter 41

There was a sense of disbelief as the train rumbled over the tracks, constantly jiggling my bunk bed in the sleeper compartment. Was I really doing this? I was jostled in the bed like a piece of bacon in a frying pan, slipping me in and out of consciousness. A series of street lamps would illuminate my window from time to time, as well as headlights from traffic on the roads the tracks would parallel.

There was the feeling of being on a momentous journey as the train passed through everyday America, from its back-yard clotheslines and laundry fluttering in the wind to its roadways and highways of cars traveling as if on their own volition. I would watch the passing scenery in the daylight from my compartment or the dining car, lost in reflection of my life's continuing narrative. I would watch the darkness of night outside the shaking train, knowing I was but a passenger being carried through a mystery.

The train pulled into the station sometime after day

broke. Several of those who de-boarded were met by others. I was met by no one. Then I realized; I was dreaming I was standing by the train. Greta was walking toward me with a sheet wrapped around her, a sheet streaked with bright red blood, as if dressed for an extreme protest rally. She was smiling though, walking toward me calling out, "Daddy."

Fast-forward, I was standing knocking on the door of a brick building and soon talking to a manager, glancing out the window to the ball field where Greta had played with the Columbia Fireflies. I learned that Gazzetti and Greta had spent a few nights here in this building of condominiums. The manager, a stately looking man with a full gray beard, looked at the photos I held up to him.

"I can never forget those two!" he said. "When they were gone, I found the bed sheets splotched with bright red blood!"

"Blood? Anyone hear commotion of any violence?"

"I can't say for sure," the manager said. "He was pretty nonchalant about it. Came to me with a fifty-dollar bill, saying the girl had gotten blood all over the sheets and hoped this would cover the cost of new ones. He was very pleasant. I saw her out the window. She looked fine. Not distraught in any way."

The sheets and the blood preyed on my mind on the trip back through the Carolinas and Virginia to Baltimore.

From Baltimore's old downtown station, I cabbed straight to Camden Yards, a sense of seeking revenge fueled by the vision of the bloody sheets and Greta's sweet smile.

I arrived unannounced, rushing by his secretary and pounding on his office door, pounding and pounding, because there was the need to vent some of the murderous rage inside me or I might kill him.

It was when I kept pounding on the door that I awoke in a hotel room, panting. The room was dark but for a slit of daylight where two curtains joined at the windows. I got out of the bed and walked to them, pulled them apart, hoping to find out where I was and wondering if I would see the green grass of Segra Park where the Columbia Fireflies play. I found instead a grand view of the Inner Harbor in all its magnificence and beyond it, Camden Yards.

There was a hard rap on the door. I looked through the peephole to see a man in a red tunic. I opened the door and saw a cart beside him and a covered plate. He was delivering a meal to the wrong room.

I sat back down on the bed, wanting to get a load off my feet as one might after a long trip. Finally, I showered, dressed, went into the hallway and to the concierge lounge where I could find eggs and bacon, smoked salmon, a roll, and coffee. I sat alone, pondering what the bloodied sheets meant. There had been no commotion during their stay in the quarters the Fireflies owner used to host out-of-town guests.

Then it dawned on me, they might have woke from their sleep in sheets soaked with blood from Greta's menstrual period. That was the logical explanation for what appeared in the dream. I never saw marks on her body that would come from being whipped or slashed by a knife.

I called Gazzetti and set up a meeting at his office for later that morning.

The intuition that drove my suspicions about Gazzetti were the same that drove my dream. They were not just fanciful creations of my mind. Pete Sake had alluded to Gazzetti having taken advantage of Greta and his ulterior motive for giving her the historical chance to play in the major leagues. Gazzetti had pimped her to all the media outlets that would end up socially raping her character. The grand finale being her *Untouchable* magazine cover. I could see him being there in the background of the photo shoot, deriving from it the same kind of pleasure a pimp gets from turning out his chick.

I found Gazzetti behind his desk, a silver tray in the middle of it offering coffee and rolls. Behind him on the wall was a framed photo of his family, wife and four kids, two of them high school age. He was known as a devout Catholic. He wore a gold chain with a gold cross round his neck matching his cuff links. He was all appearance of success and respectability.

He stood up and stretched his arm, offering his hand to shake. I maintained a civil composure and took his hand.

Chapter 42

"Have a cup of coffee," Gazzetti offered. "The almond croissant is excellent!"

I had eaten enough earlier but I wanted not to show any of the ill feelings being harbored. He poured me a cup of coffee and I reached over and put a croissant on the small plate.

"How is your beautiful family?" I asked him, glancing to the picture of his clan above his shoulder.

"Great, Tom will be a senior next year. Little Gina is taking holy communion this Sunday. Everyone is great, thanks."

"And Gina, your wife? Any more on the way?" I asked the prolific father of the Catholic faith.

"If there are, I don't know about it yet," he said, with a casual laugh. "So, what can I do for you, today, Frank?"

"Well, I just learned from one of my sources that it was you who found Greta in the sauna that afternoon."

A grim line was formed by Gazzetti's lips, as he stared at me, speechless. He began biting into the pastry roll. I thought I'd let him squirm and waited for him to respond.

He took his time chewing and swallowing and then patting his mouth with a maroon cloth napkin.

Finally, he spoke. "Yes. I found her. It was horrible. Finding her there submerged. Lifeless. I knew she had gone to the clubhouse to get her arm worked on. I wanted to give her a pep talk. She had been put through a lot in but a few weeks time. I didn't want her to be demoralized." He stopped and I could see the cogs of his wheels turning about how to proceed.

"I lifted her out of the sauna and carried her to the massage table where I tried to bring her back, blowing in her mouth, pumping her arms over her head. I was hoping, you know, I could bring her back." He spoke softly, resigned to the reality of this day. He grew silent again. I waited for him to continue but he had decided there was no more he needed to tell me.

"Who do you think killed her?" I asked, curious as to how he would answer that.

At that moment, the phone on his desk rang. He picked it up and for a minute listened and interjected with brief remarks, like "what," "when," "who," and "keep me posted." I thought it might be a police captain he was talking to and wondered how many of the brass he had gifted game tickets to. When he gave me his attention once more, I surprised him with my next question.

"When you went down to Columbia, South Carolina, on Pete Sake's tip to watch Greta pitch for the Fireflies, was she the tease the media made her out to be up here?"

"I went down there to watch her pitch. She was this little girl with a major league wind-up with tremendous control," he said, seeming to skirt the question.

"Were you able to spend any time with her down there? To get to know her, you know, what she's made of," I asked, trying another tact to draw more out of him.

I wanted to say I had been down there and talked to the manager of the quarters he shared with her. The rage inside me was forcing me to blurt it out. Fortunately, there was still enough presence of mind to realize it had been just a dream. Was it just a crazy dream? I wasn't sure.

"I spent a couple nights down there," said Gazzetti. "I took Greta to dinner after the game she pitched. She was a sweet girl who talked a lot about her daddy who'd died. She seemed to be driven by that. Her dad had taught her to pitch."

Gazzetti stopped talking and reached into his trousers and took out his gold pocket watch by its chain that was hooked to his belt loop. He looked down at the watch. I stared at it. The chain was long enough to have wrapped around Greta's neck.

He returned the watch to his pocket and looked straight at me, mulling something over in his mind.

There was a knock on the door. It pushed open and Gazzetti's secretary stuck her head in the room. "Chen is here for you, sir."

"Frank, is there anything else?" Gazzetti asked, trying to dismiss me.

I wanted to ask, "Did you kill Greta?" in some dramatic fashion. But I wimped out. I knew I did not have a sound foundation for the accusation, outside of my dream. I walked out of his room, passing the slight, Asian presence of Chen, standing a few feet from the secretary's desk.

Chapter 43

I spent the next several months on the book the commissioner had entrusted me to write. It wasn't easy. After the first few weeks, I felt disoriented. I shredded my work in progress and reluctantly turned down an invitation from Lin Pi to be his guest for the games in China.

I was having trouble reconciling a narrative on Greta's time in the majors that omitted my relationship with her. When I tried doing so it was like a big hole existed in the story, a painful gap in the truth of the account. So, I spent a month writing poetry about her. This got all the pain out of my system and onto a page, one poem at a time. A lot of it was a celebration of what once was and a lot was trying to understand what we were together beyond the sex. This was the elusive element. Without the intense physical attraction defining the relationship, all the recollections of our moments were faded or shallow, at least in contrast.

So, I wrote another baseball book. I described Greta's life as she had told it to me. I described her discipline in the art of pitching a baseball. I described the many examples of how she pitched with finesse at a low plane the batters found it hard adjusting to. I played back the games she won and the trouble with Hanger. I detailed how she was beloved by the media at first only to be turned on in the vilest way possible. How she was misunderstood by a media that wasn't into understanding anything or anybody. How she was set up by TV hosts and by *Untouchable*. How Gazzetti's strategy for publicity backfired on him and major league baseball.

I told the story of Antonelli's leadership, how he had seized on the moment with Gazzetti calling up Greta to join the Baseball Club, how he asked me to play the sleuth, the many suspects in the murder investigation, and lastly the Chinese intrigue. I wasn't sure how he would take that episode in the book.

I told the story how Greta made a lot of money for the Baltimore Baseball Club and the entry of sex into the big league game, from the slit up Greta's uniform to her penchant for super-short skirts, flouting her great legs. That was the long chapter. I called it, "Legs." It could help mushroom book sales to the *New York Times* best-seller list.

Kate often called me but it wasn't until after I finished the book that I saw her again. I had wanted to be alone, until I couldn't stand it anymore.

Being alone without a woman is not a settled state of being for me. I need a woman's character and charm to bounce off, to feel who I am. I am not at home with only myself. That is, unless I am writing.

The first time Kate visited me in Hoboken was like a reunion with a high school sweetheart. We walked, held hands, spoke about what we were reading and writing these days, and talked about the past season we both experienced. Having dinner at my kitchen table we got to talking about the murder.

"Buffalo Bob was sure it was Riobonito's lover."

"Didn't they interrogate him only to let him go?" Kate asked.

"I think maybe his only crime was that he was wound too tight. I don't see how those two could stay together after Juan reported him to the police."

"Who else did Buffalo Bob believe was the killer?" Kate asked, chuckling.

"Everyone was a killer in Bob's mind," I said. "Even Chen."

Chen was one of the security men at Camden Yards Bob had questioned, the same Chen that called to alert Kate to Greta's death. He learned that Chen had a family back in the mainland, that he'd been in the U.S. for almost two decades. When I told Bob of the Chinese being unhappy with a female breaking into the majors, a nefarious plot began weaving in his big head. "They ordered Chen to eliminate her," he said, suddenly sure of his quick-spun theory.

I had this conversation with Buffalo Bob before I left Baltimore, about the Chinese reaction to Greta in the big leagues, when he said something that set my head spinning. I relayed it to Kate.

"What's that?" asked Kate, taking a sip of the red wine from her glass.

"He said the Chinese would have come around to Greta playing. 'She's chopsticks,' he said. 'They would have seen that,' he said. Then, 'They might have given the order too hastily.'"

"I said, 'What did you say, Bob? Chopsticks?' 'Chopsticks,' he said. 'Chinese have the finesse. That's what pitching is about. Yep, the chinks would have come around to her.'" The guy had an off-color label for every ethnic group: polaks, krauts, limeys.

"The thing about baseball and chopsticks, that's what China's Chairman Wong would say, according to Lin Pi. Wong compared the deft use of chopsticks to the art of swinging a bat. Now here was Bob with the same analogy."

"Maybe," said Kate, "He visited the Great Hall of China and ran into Wong."

"Maybe. Maybe he rode his bike all the way to China."

Both of us burst out laughing, the wine having injected absurdity into our humor.

"When's the trial going to start?" I asked Kate.

"Next month, I think."

"You think they'll convict her?"

Kate turned both palms of her hands up. "It's all circumstantial evidence, isn't it? Pictures of Greta on the wall, her ritual of using a choke chain on her girlfriend."

"Yeah, they might as well put Monk Morton on trial for walking his Rottweiler with a choke collar."

"Or Gazzetti," Kate said, pouring us both more wine from the bottle.

We toasted, clinking our glasses together: "Or Gazzetti!"

We sipped the wine and stared at each other, some puzzle still in our eyes.

"You know, Kate, Tom Grazer doesn't even think Grendel did it."

We sat then, all chain of thought interrupted and nothing filling the void.

"Hey," Kate said, a new thought ready to float out over her wine glass. "Maybe Grendel's girlfriend did it."

I tilted my head and wondered why I hadn't thought of that one. Maybe the killer, indeed, was someone no one ever suspected.

I poured out the last of the bottle.

Later, in bed, we focused just on the two of us. This, I figured out late in life, was the secret to good sex and a lasting relationship. Kate fell asleep with her head resting along my side and her long hair splayed across her shoulder and back. The light of the moon shown through the gauzy curtains onto the bed. I could see and feel the woman beside me.

A.T. ARMADA

The End

A.T. ARMADA

Acknowledgements

My thanks to Charles, and George for their editorial roles on this book, and to the wizard, Ryan, for all his formatting assistance.

I am also thankful for Sally and Justine in helping me to have the strength and the time to write this story.

Lastly, a nod and a smile to the girl who throws like a boy.